Ghosting

Ghosting

EDITH PATTOU

SKYSCAPE

SKYSCAPE

Published by Skyscape, New York

www.apub.com

Amazon, the Amazon logo, and Skyscape are trademarks of Amazon.com, Inc., or its affiliates.

ISBN-13: 9781477847749 (hardcover)
ISBN-10: 147784774X (hardcover)
ISBN-13: 9781477847893 (paperback)
ISBN-10: 1477847898 (paperback)

Grateful acknowledgement is made to Farrar, Straus and Giroux for permission to quote from JOEY PIGZA LOSES CONTROL © 2000 by Jack Gantos. Reprinted by permission of Farrar, Straus and Giroux Books for Young Readers. All rights reserved.

Book design by Abby Kuperstock
Cover design by Greg Stadnyk

Library of Congress Control Number: 2014933207

Printed in the United States of America

To Robert,
who played Mouse Trap with me and
who I will miss forever,
and
to Charles and Vita, as always.

White bird,
crisply folded,
wings its way
    into Spring.

E. P.

Ghosting

MAXIE

When I was a little girl
ghosting was
a sheet of paper and
a drawing in
     black ink.

A crudely sketched ghost,
with a Tootsie Roll
     taped on.

Not scary.

A fun Halloween prank.
You slipped it under a
neighbor's door,
ran away,
          giggling.

"You've been ghosted!"

Exciting.
Harmless.

But now
ghosting is:

          this can't be happening,
          screams like knives in your ears,
          pooling glistening blood.
          Everywhere.
          And death, bellowing
          hot and loud
                    in
                    your
                    face.

BEFORE

FAITH

At the
kitchen table,
eating cereal.
Puffins,
my favorite,
pillowy
with a soft
milky
crunch.

The sun
glares
through
the window,
reflecting off
the stainless-
steel dishwasher.

Even though
my bare feet
are cold
from the
air-conditioning,
I can tell it's
hot outside
already.

Mom is
at the sink,
rinsing bottles
for recycling.
Polly, our
big black dog
who needs
a haircut,
lies under
the table,
drowsing.
I stick my toes
under her belly
to warm them.

Peaceful.
Then
Emma bursts in,
noisy
and rushed
like always.

Have you seen a hair band? I need a hair band,
right now!

Everything is
"right now"
for Emma.

I'm so freaking late! she says.

Polly bounds
up from
under
the table,
tail wagging
a hundred miles
an hour,
panting.

Mom's back
tightens.

> *Emma, you were late last night. Past your curfew . . . ,*
>   she says.
> *Not now, Mom.*

Emma's
voice is
sharp.

> *Coach is going to kill me.*

She grabs
a protein bar,
her water bottle,
and she's gone
with a flash of
dark-red ponytail.

Polly circles

the table
a few times,
then settles back
underneath,
at my feet,
with a gentle
disappointed
sigh.
Mom turns
on the
faucet again,
picks up a
Gatorade bottle,
only now
her shoulders
are slumped,
tired-looking.

Is Emma going to be grounded? I ask.
Your dad and I are going to talk to her.

Which means
no.

Dad is soft
on Emma;
well, we all are,
because we love her
so much,
but especially
Dad.

Mom worries
about it.
I've heard
them argue.

I spoon
a Puffin
into my
mouth.
The crunch
is gone.

Polly sighs
against
my feet.
I swallow
the soggy
Puffin, past
the lump
in my
throat.

MAXIE

It wasn't hot like this
in Colorado,
even though
we were a mile closer
    to the sun.

I forgot about Midwest heat,
like a steamy-wet-hot washcloth
pressed against your mouth and nose.

And the air conditioner
is busted.

    Maxine, Mom says (she's the only person who calls
    me that), *I'm going stark raving crazy in this heat.*

The making-mom-crazy list is long,
and number one,
at the tip-top of the list is:
    my dad.

His chewing too loud.
His interrupting when she's on the phone.
His beer drinking.
I could go on.

But most crazy-making of all,

the fact that
he dragged us out to Colorado
for four years
for this fabulous job opportunity
that turned out to be a bust.
    A big bust.

So here we are,
back in the house where I grew up,
the house that
was never sold
for four years,
which also drove my mom nuts.

Of course now it's a nightmare turned
    blessing in disguise.

My mom is little-miss-busy,
getting the house fixed up,
enrolling in nursing classes
to update her skills.

    Someone's got to have a steady income, she says.

And she says it with all kinds of
righteousness.
Not meaning to hurt,
but wounding just the same.

My dad is still recognizable as my dad,

just a flat, joyless version.
Like a light has
    gone out.

Except when he's drinking his beers.
Then he gets jolly and sweet,
                which almost
                makes me
                look forward
                to that pop-squelch
                of the flip-top on
                the Miller can.
        Almost.

ANIL

1. Wednesday morning, 7:30 a.m.:
    I am alone in the house,
    eating leftover lentils and rice,
    heated in the microwave.
    I stand over the sink,
    looking out the window at the back lawn,
    perfectly mowed and trimmed
    by my father last night before dinner.

2. Father:
    Dr. Sanjeev Sayanantham,
    who left for Highland Park Hospital
    at five this morning,
    who was named
    by *U.S. News & World Report*
    as one of the top ten best hand surgeons
    in the country.

    Dr. Sayanantham,
    famous not only for his skill in the operating room,
    but also for his charisma,
    not stiff like a lot of Indian physicians.
    And you'd never know he was born in Calcutta
    the way he's smoothed out his accent.

3. Mother:
    Dr. Rahel Sayanantham,

who also left early this morning
for her thriving practice as a pediatrician.

This Dr. Sayanantham does have a wisp of an accent,
even though she is only half Indian.
Her father was a handsome white dentist
who married Grandmother Rumma
against the wishes of her family.

Mom lived in Mumbai until she came
to the US for medical school,
where she met my dad.
According to family lore
he was swept away
from the very moment he saw her:
black-eyed, black-haired beauty
with a gentle voice.
Small, too, like a strong gust of wind
could blow her away.

4. Brother:
    Viraj Sayanantham
    born when my mother
    was doing her residency at the University of Michigan.
    Viraj hasn't lived at home for six years
    and is himself a Neurology resident
    at Mass General, in Boston.

    Viraj is the golden son
    who prefers Christmas to Diwali,

cheeseburgers to lentils and rice.
He will be Dr. Sayanantham number three.

5.   Me:
Son number two.
Expected to be
Dr. Sayanantham number four.
And even though, yes,
science and math come easy,
I love words, too.

And I don't know if I wish to follow
in the footsteps of my
cheeseburger-loving brother.

The end result, these simple
but puzzling equations:

$a \leq b$
or
$a \geq b$
or
$a \neq b$

a being what is expected of me
b being where my heart lies
x being an unknown quantity
utilized to figure out the intersection
between them, assuming I ever
find out what b actually is.

EMMA

I down a tall glass of Cran-Apple
with crushed ice, too fast,
but I can't help it.

It tastes so good, cold and tart,
filling what feels like
a bottomless thirst.

I am exhilarated, wrung out,
but keyed up,
from an amazing practice.

I love that feeling
after I've pushed my body
to its limit.

It's nice to have the kitchen to myself.
No nagging from Mom.
No questions from Faith.

Sweet Faith, who watches me like a hawk,
which can get annoying, sometimes,
like she's memorizing me.

I like the quiet, but I miss Polly
banging her tail against my sweaty legs,
drooling and panting love all over me.

Mom and Faith must've taken
her with them on their
last week-before-school-starts errands.

It's Faith's first year at the high school
and even though quiet is her style,
I can tell Faith is pumped.

I don't remember feeling like that,
except for maybe the first time
I went to soccer camp.

It was the summer before 8th grade.
I remember making out with the
cute, blond assistant coach.

A total rush, until he got clingy
toward the end.
Which was awkward.

But high school, no.
I'm so done with high school.
Can't wait to play soccer at Penn.

I wish I could wave a wand
and whoosh away
the next nine months.

My cell buzzes with a text
from Brendan. Damn, I still haven't

told him about Saturday night.

About how we have to drag
Maxie Kalman along with us.
Thanks to my mom.

Saw Mrs. Kalman in the grocery store, Mom said. *Poor*
thing, she looked miserable. I told her you'd include
Maxie in your plans this weekend. She was so grateful.

Maybe I'll see if I can get Felix
to join us, for old time's sake.
Brendan doesn't mind Felix.

Who could mind Felix?
Not the winner he used to be,
but still a good kid.

Maxie and I and Felix were tight
back when we were kids.
Lemonade stands, kickball, the whole bit.

But that was a long time ago.
I hope she isn't too weird now.
She always was the artistic type.

Whatever.
As long as she doesn't ruin
Saturday night.

CHLOE

"I Am/I Am Not"

My mom is big into personal inventories.
Back when Dad dumped her
and right before she became a realtor,
she stocked up on all these self-help books
and they all told her
to make a list of who she is
and who she hopes to be.

She's always trying to get me
to do them, but I always refuse.
They remind me of those "I am" poems
we did back in 5th grade.

I am *cheerful and tan.*
I wonder *if I will ever finish this poem.*
I hear *the sound of one hand clapping.*
I see *rainbows and unicorns.*
I want *a boyfriend and a new smartphone.*
I am *cheerful and tan.*

Okay, I don't think that's really
what I wrote in 5th grade,
but close.

So here's my up-to-date, honest,
anti personal inventory.

What I'm <u>not</u>:

    a cheerleader.

    a soccer player, or a jock of any kind.

    an art nerd.

    a math and science nerd.

    a Christian nerd.

    a drama geek.

    a *Harry Potter* freak.

Oh, and I'm <u>not</u>:

    smart.

    quick with a comeback.

    careful.

What I <u>am</u>:

    a klutz.

    pretty.

    cheerful, or at least decent at faking it.

What I am good at:

    babysitting.

    picking out clothes.

    makeup.

    blow-drying,

    showering, and exfoliating.

    cleaning my room.

    sex.

What I'm not good at:

    just about everything else.

MAXIE

Mom kept at me about Emma,
to call her just as soon
as we moved back.

You two were best friends, Mom said.
That was a long time ago, I answered.

I kept putting it off.
It's not like we stayed in touch
while I was gone.
She's the one who faded away,
  stopped writing,
  stopped calling.

She's probably too busy with soccer, Mom would say.

Yeah, right.
But I understood,
  life goes on.

It's not like we can
just pick up
where we left off.
But to get Mom
  off my back
I sent Emma
an e-mail.

A few days later:

> Jeez, sorry, I just saw this. Never look at e-mail,
> what's your cell? I'll text :)

But she didn't.

Then my mom ran into her mom
at the grocery store.
After that Emma texted me.

> Sorry!! Crazy busy. Free Sat night?
> Can't wait to see you!

Yeah, right.

ANIL

1. Girlfriend:
    Chloe Carney,
    for the past month and a half.
    At least I think she is.
    The code for these things
    mystifies me in a way that
    math equations
    never do.

    Especially since I've never
    had a girlfriend before.

    And what kind of dumb luck is it
    that Chloe Carney should be my first.
    Chloe Carney, with her looks that stop traffic.
    Literally.
    (I saw a pickup truck
    rear-end an SUV last week.
    On account of Chloe Carney
    and her blue sundress.)

2. Let's be honest:
    I am not Chloe Carney's usual type.

    I'm
    <u>not</u> good-looking,

not a lacrosse player,
not white.

3. How it began:
After teaching junior clinics all morning
Zander and I were goofing around on the
tennis courts.
Some kid from the community pool
next to the courts kept hollering "Marco Polo"
in this high-pitched pirate accent
that cracked Zander up.
So I kept hammering his backhand.
Beat him 6–0.

I didn't even notice Chloe Carney
watching through the chain-link, but Zander did.
At the changeover he told me a hot blonde
was checking me out.

I didn't believe him. Looked over,
but she was gone by then.

But later, when Zander and I were leaving,
this girl from my class, with honey-blonde hair,
was hanging out by the tennis shop.

Chloe Carney.
I knew her name because she's one of those girls
whose name you just know, everyone knows.

She said something dumb like
   Hey, Mr. Six-Pack.

I don't usually play without a shirt,
but it was blistering hot that day
and I was soaked through
and I'd had this reckless so-what feeling,
so I stripped off my shirt after the first set.

Reckless.
Good word
when it comes to describing how
Chloe Carney makes me feel.

She said she'd seen me at the high school
and wasn't I on the tennis team and what was
my name?

I said Anil. Then introduced her to Zander.
He's on the team, too.
But she didn't seem to care.

   Hey, Anil, Zander said, *let's go. I gotta get home.*
   Nice meeting you, Anil, Chloe Carney said.

Polite words.
But she said my name like it was
some exotic, mouthwatering candy
from World Market.

4. That weekend:
    a party at a kid's house,
    and Chloe was there.
    She and her friend Emma came up to me.

        This is Anil who's a tennis player, Chloe said,
        and he's ripped.

    Emma rolled her eyes and then eased away,
    calling someone's name.

        I couldn't take my eyes off you, Chloe said in a
        husky, flirty voice.

    Then she laughed,
    and I laughed back.

5. How could I say no to Chloe Carney?
    How could anyone?
    She is one of the prettiest girls I've ever seen.
    Hair the color of clover honey,
    with all sorts of shifting lights in it.
    Deep blue eyes.
    Royal blue.

    I haven't brought Chloe Carney home,
    but my parents know about her.
    The only thing my father said,

        It's okay to have fun, Anil, but be careful.
        Use protection.

Which made me blush,
but he was using his white-coat doctor voice
so it was okay.

And remember, he went on, *once school starts
you're going to be busy.*

6.   Busy, yes.
My senior year:

Tennis team captain
School newspaper editor
AP classes
International Baccalaureate
College applications, more than one, in case, God forbid,
I don't get into Columbia.

7.   But sometimes it's nice
to feel
no pressure.

Just be
reckless,
with Chloe Carney.

MAXIE

I am not ready to walk
through the doors to
George Washington High School
on Monday morning.
Even though
when I was
a kid I
couldn't wait.

In middle school I'd walk by
George Washington High School,
watching kids in their hoodies
and ratty sneakers,
smoking cigarettes,
swearing at each other.
            I wanted that.

I still remember the day Mom
told me we were moving to Colorado
and I'd be going to high school
at some place called East High,
which I had never seen
and where I wouldn't know
            a single person.

I felt cheated,
betrayed.

Like my parents had
stolen my future.

But it wasn't so bad.
I made a few friends,
learned how to ski,
and, most important,
had this awesome teacher,
Mrs. Gablowski.

She's the one who put
a camera in my hands
for the first time
and told me I was a natural:
        observer,
        composer,
        finder of moments.

So here I am, back again.
A senior.
At George Washington High School.

I feel like I'm going
the wrong way in a
        revolving door.

I'll know people
but not really.
And they'll know me
but not really.

I'll have to start over,
figuring out where I fit in.
Which tribe will take me in?

I'll probably end up
an art geek
because of
　　　the camera.

But the whole prospect,
of starting over
as new/old girl,
is terrifying.

Emma texted today, saying,

　　　We're on for Saturday night.

She even listed who'll be there:
　　　Her boyfriend, Brendan, who I never knew,
　　　　　different middle school,
　　　　　different crowd.
　　　Chloe Carney.
　　　　　Friend of Emma's from middle school days,
　　　　　when Emma and I began drifting apart.
　　　Chloe's boyfriend.
　　　　　No name.
　　　Felix, former best bud.
　　　　　Which makes me happy.
　　　　　Very happy.

Emma, Felix, and Max.
An elementary school trio.
      Legendary.

"EMFAX" is what Dad dubbed us,
and it stuck.

When we were kids
everyone loved
      Felix.

He was the only boy
invited to all the girls' birthday parties.
Not because he was a girly guy,
not at all.
He was a big soccer nut.
But because he was just
so darn
cute.

Neither of us was
good at keeping in touch
after I moved
to Colorado,
but it'll be great to see him.
I remember how he used to
bound up to everyone,
all high energy,
with that immediate
big grin.

Anyway, I guess Saturday night
will be a good first
        toe in the water.

Hopefully I'll still have all my toes
when the night's
done.

FELIX

i flick the switch of the kitchen light. nothing. bulb must
be busted. and i used the last bulb when i changed the one
in mom's reading lamp a few weeks ago. not that she reads
anymore. most nights she falls asleep watching tv.

so it's cheerios in the dark for dinner again. solo, naturally,
since mom is asleep by now. but it's not a bad routine.
i've always been a cereal-for-dinner fan. didn't expect it'd
happen most nights like this, but it's cool.

no clean bowls though and the milk smells off. that sucks.
i wish mom didn't have to work so hard. and that she was
happy. the way she was happy when i was a kid.

she had a lot of energy then, which was a good thing since
i was a real nutso, revved-up kid, because of the adhd. she
was always game for running after me, always patient with
the calls from school about the busted fish tank, missing
gerbil, library books in the boys' bathroom toilets. etc. not
dad. he wasn't patient. but mom didn't believe in meds and
said she'd hang in there with me. all the time. and she did.

until lately.

yeah, lately she's pretty much checked out. but i understand.
and i can cut her some slack, after all the slack she's cut me.

tomorrow's my last day at the library. community service

for being busted for pot end of last year. best part was working in the kids' section. tomorrow we'll have a few stragglers, kids wanting prizes for the summer reading program, which ended a week ago. that nice librarian, mrs. sheridan, with hair so long she can sit on it, she'll give them prizes anyway.

mrs. sheridan was around back when emma, max, and i did the summer reading program. that's when i discovered the joey pigza books by jack gantos. i liked joey pigza because he was like me, only worse. i must've read the first one about twenty times. and good old mrs. sheridan counted each time as a separate book, so i'd get the prizes.

maybe tomorrow i'll check out a joey pigza book. for old time's sake.

weird that emma invited me to hang out with her and her friends saturday night. weird that it'll be emma, max, and me together again. EMFAX. crazy. haven't thought about EMFAX in a long time. stoked to see max though. takes me back, to when things were a whole lot simpler.

BRENDAN

Last weekend before the grind starts up again.
Down for some serious fun.

Why the hell does Emma have to drag along
this girl nobody knows on Saturday night?

> *She'd better not be a loser, or a buzzkill,* I say.
> *Be nice,* Emma says. *My mom made me.*
> *We can always ditch her,* I say.

And Emma smiles,
so I know it's cool.

Felix is okay,
long as he's not too baked.

And Chloe's all right,
always up for some fun.

But what's the deal with this Anil guy?
It's not like I'm a racist or anything.

Maybe it's the brainiac thing.
Mr. National Merit Scholar.

He's in all the AP classes;
he probably hangs with the geeks.

Seen him in the workout room.
Watching and looking around all the time.

Probably looking down on the rest of us.
Screw that.

Wish Chloe had stuck with Josh.
Even though he's a dick, I get Josh.

CHLOE

"Senior Year"

I'm totally sick of scooping
ice cream at Bonnie's Sweet Shop
My fingers—always sticky.
And Lou, the manager, always hitting on me.
But it still sucks that school
starts on Monday.

Mom keeps saying
I need a 2.9,
if I want to go to
Illinois State.

Who said I want to;
it's her who's always wanted me
to go there.
All because *she* went
to Illinois State,
best freaking four years of her life.

Downhill ever since,
if you ask me.

Poor mom:
    single mom.
    3 kids.
    husband long gone.

(Would never want her life. Not. Ever.)
Lucky dad:
>cute new younger wife.
>black-haired, dimply baby girl.
>big house in California.
(Who cares.)

Dad's been gone
since I was in 6th grade.
Mom clawed her way
up in the real estate business.
Has her own company now,
and her plastic face
is on the back page
of our town newspaper
every week,
not to mention plastered
on benches all around town.
My smiley-face mom
holding an umbrella:
>*"I'm On Your Side,*
>*Come Rain Or Come Shine"*

Gag me.

At least there's Anil now.
Good, real,
hot-bod Anil.

Maybe senior year
won't be all bad.

FAITH

I love
riding
my bike
around town.
Today I
take Polly
because
she's restless,
on edge.
I know
she is
because
so am I.

And the
reason
is that
Mom and Dad
have been
yelling at
each other
all morning.
About Emma,
of course.

Mom thinks
they should be
stricter,

but Dad says
no.

Emma should have fun.
Brendan's a good kid.
She'll be off to college soon, needs to get used to
her freedom.

I get
where Dad's
coming from.
On the
other hand,
he's wrong
about
Brendan.
Even in
middle school,
kids told
stories
about him,
crazy stuff
he's done.
But he's
a jock, and
good-looking,
so he gets
away with
everything.

Still, Emma
knows

how to
handle him,
the way
she knows
how to
handle
everything.

Although
one night
this summer
she came
home
upset.
Some
stupid prank
he pulled
that went
a little
too far.
    Almost got us killed, she said.

But she
said it
angry,
not scared.
Emma doesn't
get scared.
Not the way
most people
do.

One good thing
about Emma is
she always
tells me
the truth.
Any question
I ask.
She said
it's because
I need to know
the way things
really are,
not the bullshit
you get from
parents
and teachers
and movies
and TV.

So she's told
me all about
the sex
she's had,
the drugs
she's tried.

She says
I'm smart
like her
and won't
get carried

away by
any of it.

I'm thinking
about Emma
and Brendan
again,
wondering
what he
did that
almost got
them killed,
when I
realize I've
come to
the front
gates of
Walnut Creek
Cemetery.
I slow down,
and Polly
slows, too.

Slanting rays
of the sun
send long
black stripes
along the
green cemetery
grass,
shadows

from the
grave markers
in their
straight rows.
I stop to look.
Rubbing
Polly's ears
with one hand,
I shade
my eyes
with the
other, and
think about
Emma again.

And I
realize
that I
am
smart
like her.
Actually,
maybe
smarter.

Because
I would never
get involved
with a boy
like Brendan.

WALTER

Looking down from my window,
    I watch Mother hunched over,
kneeling in her garden.
    Working all the time on her roses.

She looks old, bent, confused sometimes.
    Found a pile of dirty dishes
in the freezer yesterday.
    But I'll take care of her.

She always took care of me.
    Watching over me, protecting me from bad guys.
Read to me every night. Cowboy stories.
    My favorites, over and over.

Then I see a movement by the cemetery
    down the block, and look over.
I get nervous when I see people there
    because it's either someone sad with flowers,

Or it's one of the bad guys,
    the people who pester us.
But this time I see that it's just
    a girl on a bike.

She's got a dog with her, a large soft-looking dog,
    and she's petting it.

I can tell she loves her dog
    and her dog loves her.

Even though she's far away and I can't see her face,
    she looks nice,
like someone who could be a friend.
    If I had friends.

Then I see her get back on her bike and
    ride off, her dog running beside her.
Her ponytail flies out behind her, like that
    tattered wind sock Mother put up a long time ago.

I'm feeling good, not lonely.
    And then a car drives by, slowly.
I hear a muffled shout and a whistle,
    and then Mother yelling back, angry.

I get angry, too. And I wish the bad guys
    would just leave us alone.
If everyone would leave us alone,
    except nice girls like that one with her dog,
we'd be okay.

POLICE CHIEF AUBREY DELAFIELD

Quiet day. Which is a good thing
since all hell's gonna break loose,
starting tonight.

Weekend before school starts.
All those high school kids,
spoiled kids with too much time on their hands,
gotta blow off steam.

Some girl will end up in the ER
from too many shots of Jägermeister,
swearing to her parents it's the first time she ever tried it.
And they'll believe her,
God help 'em.
Some boys will go joyriding out on Highway 54
or drag racing down Central.

Worst was back in '86,
before my time:
three seventeen-year-old boys dead,
Dad's Jaguar wrapped around a century-old oak tree.

Me, I've been lucky,
knock wood.
Nobody's died,
not on my watch.
Not yet.

MAXIE

I try on about ten different combinations of
jeans and shirts,
skirts and tees,
which is so stupid,
because it really doesn't matter
    what I wear.

It'll be lame compared to
Emma and
    Chloe the gorgeous.

I put on some old jeans
and my lavender shirt,
the one I wore for the unofficial
good-bye–to–Colorado party
my best friend Mandy threw together
at the last minute.
Which was fantastic
    and sad
and awkward,
    all at once.

Dad is just back
from the grocery store.

He's piled all the canvas tote bags
on the counter

and Mom is helping him
put groceries away
and I'm thinking this is a
cozy domestic scene,
tranquil even,
until Mom pulls out a six-pack
of amber

> long-
> necked
> beer
> bottles
> with
> orange
> labels.

What's this? she asks, frowning.
This, says Dad, with a silly grin, *is some seriously
    fine summer ale.*
We can't afford fancy-schmancy summer ale,
    says Mom.
*Oh, come on, Glory. We need to celebrate the end
    of summer.*

He slides an arm
around her waist,
but Mom dodges it,
her lips tight.
Dad reaches into a drawer for
a bottle opener.

The sound isn't the same as

the metallic pop-squelch of a can.
This is more of a
  long
  cool
  hissing
  noise.

He slips out the back door,
beer in hand.

Mom sighs.

> *Are you having dinner with us, Maxine?* she asks.
> *No, thanks,* I say. *Emma said we'd probably grab a*
>   *bite somewhere.*
> *You look nice,* says Mom, her eyes softening. *I'm so*
>   *glad you're spending the evening with Emma. Just like*
>   *old times.*

Did I mention
how moms can be
  clueless?

Dad reappears.
And I can't help spotting that
the beer bottle is almost
empty.
  Already.

> *Hey, Dad, can you give me a ride to Emma's?* I say

quickly, hoping my mom isn't noticing what I
just noticed.
Of course, Maxie-bean, he answers.

Dad has about
a million nicknames
for me.

Mom and I watch
as he polishes off the rest of his
fine summer ale.

Let's go, bread-face, he says.

Honestly, who calls their kid
bread-face?
But truth is
I love it.

Reminds me of being a kid,
eating sugar sandwiches
with squishy white bread and butter.
That's when he first
started calling me
bread-face,
when sugar sandwiches were
my favorite food
in the entire world
and I wanted them for
every meal.

Have fun, Maxine, says Mom.

As we drive
Dad shoots me
a sideways glance.

Don't worry, bean, he says.
About what? I ask, surprised.
Anything, he answers with a grin.

Dad has always
been able to read
  my face.

Okay, who am I kidding.
Most people can read
  my face.
Face control is not
my strong suit.

But suddenly,
I have this feeling,
a shivery foreboding sort of feeling,
that tonight,
with Emma,
I'm going to need all
the face control I can manage.

EMMA

Up in my bedroom I can smell
cinnamon and oats, from the cookies
Faith baked earlier.

The AC is on, but I've got
the window open.
I like the heat.

Brendan wanted our last Saturday night
before school to be with his lacrosse buddies,
so he's mad at me.

Too bad. But the best part
will be after anyway.
When it is just us two.

I like it with Brendan, especially
the way he kisses me.
He's good at kissing.

It surprised me the first time.
Soft and sweet and kind of eager.
Not like I expected.

And I've always liked Bren best when
we're alone. Otherwise he can be an asshole,
all Mr. Cool, life of the party.

I guess that's because of his messed-up dad.
He never talks about his dad.
But I've seen.

It'd be a bummer to have a dad like that,
who expects, no, *demands*,
that his son be Perfect.

Just so he can tell all his buddies
what a "great fucking son"
he has.

And his mom is like a shadow.
Beautiful and country-club perfect,
but barely there.

I know I'm lucky.
I love how my dad
loves me.

And even though my mom can be a bitch,
ragging me all the time about curfew,
I know she loves me too.

I promised her I'd get home on time tonight.
But it's the last weekend before school.
So screw that.

BRENDAN

I head down to the garage, grabbing
car keys off the hook in the kitchen.

My little brother, Bobby, is at the kitchen counter,
bent over papers spread out on the black granite.

> *Yo, Bobby, it's Saturday night,* I say. *Plenty of time to
> crack the books tomorrow.*

He smiles and jumps off the stool,
following me out to the garage.

> *What's today, Bobby?* I ask

It's a running joke we have since Bobby
found this book at the library.

It's got all these weird holidays in it
and Bobby thinks it's great.

> *It's Race Your Mouse Day,* he says with an ear-to-ear
>   grin.
> *No shit,* I say. *Too bad we don't have one. But Happy
>   Race Your Mouse Day, big guy.*
> *You, too,* Bobby answers.

I grab a few plastic bags I'd hidden
behind some old ice skates.

They're mine from a long time ago.
I've logged a lot of ice time on those skates.

> *What's that?* Bobby asks, watching me carry the bags
> to the car.
> *Just some stuff I'm taking to the party we're going to.*
> *You and your girlfriend?* he asks.

He says the word girlfriend in that teasing,
exaggerated way kids do.

But he likes Emma,
has right from the start.

> *Yep,* I say. *And a few friends.*

I open the door of the SUV,
stick the bags and a cooler inside.

> *Robert! ROBERT DONNELLY!*

It's Dad's voice, coming
from inside the house.

Bobby's face gets that
paralyzed look I know so well.

Then Dad appears in the garage doorway.
He looks pissed. Damn.

Robert, you get your ass back to that kitchen counter.
Now!

Bobby doesn't move right away and in seconds
Dad is at his side, grabbing his arm.

I can see his fingers biting
into Bobby's tanned skin.

Hey, Dad, I say, *it was my fault. I asked Bobby to*
help with . . .

He turns to me,
frowning.

Don't make excuses for your brother, he barks. *Robert*
knew he wasn't to leave the table until he finished his
assignment.
But . . . , I start.

Dad is already yanking Bobby
out of the garage.

Dad . . . , I start again, following them.
You stay the fuck out of this, Dad says without even
looking at me.

He shoves Bobby toward the granite counter,
and Bobby quickly climbs onto the chair.

I can see the white marks where Dad's
fingers grasped Bobby's arm.

Bobby looks over at me,
gives me a shaky grin.

> *Have fun with your girlfriend,* he says.
> *Thanks,* I say. *I'll wish her a happy Mouse Day for you.*
> *Happy Race Your Mouse Day,* Bobby says,
>   correcting me.

Dad is standing there, arms folded,
watching Bobby until he picks up his pen.

It isn't until I'm sitting behind the wheel,
turning the key in the ignition,

when I suddenly remember,
clear as a bell.

The first time Dad hit me.
I was just Bobby's age.

ANIL

1. I know I should wear a T-shirt and
baggy cargo shorts.
That's what the other guys
will be wearing tonight.

For Christmas Viraj gave me
a couple of T-shirts from rock concerts
he'd been to in Boston.
Foo Fighters and Death Cab for Cutie.
Either would probably be perfect.
But I can't.

2. And it's not because of the disapproving look
I would inevitably get from my father.

> *These American teenagers are so disrespectful*, he
> says frequently.

No, it's because of some deficiency in me.
When I put the Foo Fighters T-shirt on
and gaze in the mirror,
I look like an impostor,
with my Indian eyes and brown skin
and black hair.
Viraj can pull it off.
Me, I look like I'm trying too hard.

3. Chloe is going to meet my parents tonight,

for the first time.
She arranged it that way,
for her friends to pick us up here.
I'm not sure why.
Maybe to put some kind of
official stamp on us,
before school starts on Monday.

4. I decide to keep the cargo shorts on,
   but put away the T-shirts,
   neatly folded in my dresser,
   and pull on a blue sport shirt.

   It isn't every day that your parents
   meet your first girlfriend
   for the first time.

CHLOE

"Things We Carry"

I love that feature in *Us Weekly* magazine
where they list all the stuff
in some celebrity's purse.

It's like you get clues to what kind of a
person she is,
plus you get good tips on makeup
and other stuff.

There was one a few weeks ago
from an old TV star who said she
always carries:
  a vibrator and
  a statue of St. Francis,
which is totally hilarious.

Here's what's in *my* purse for
the last Saturday night before
school starts:

1. *Hello Kitty change purse*
2. *Flowerbomb perfume*
3. *Cherry ChapStick (I'm an addict.)*
4. *Stila starfruit lip glaze*
5. *Stride gum Nonstop Mint*

6. *Listerine Cool Mint Pocketmist*
7. *Cell phone*
8. *Hand sanitizer (I'm a little nuts about germs.)*
9. *Condom (A girl can hope, even though Anil hasn't wanted to. Yet.)*

FELIX

mom and i are at the kitchen table, finishing our take-out
dinner. mom's been obsessed with chicken tenders lately.
she says they're healthier than burgers, but if you look it
up, i don't think so. she sure likes all the dipping sauces,
honey mustard being her favorite.

i can see dad's latest letter lying on the kitchen counter. she
must've been rereading it while i made the food run. she
starts to tell me he's okay and in a safer part of afghanistan.
i tune her out while i put our plates in the sink. so she
switches to another topic, asking what my plans are for
tonight. i tell her i'm seeing emma and maxie, who's just
moved back to town, and her face lights up. haven't seen
that in a while.

> *That's nice,* she sighs, her eyes unfocused and on
> some distant memory. *Maxie was such a cute little girl.*

then mom moves slowly toward the family room and the
tv. i notice she looks a little thicker and puffier than she
used to. must be the sleeping pills she takes. and all those
chicken tenders.

> *Don't stay out too late,* she calls to me before switching
> on the tv set.

not that she'd notice how late i stay out, the way those pills
knock her out.

Okay, Mom, i call back, and head up to my room to roll a few joints.

EMFAX. crazy to think about after all these years. always sounded like a corporation to me, like fedex or amtrak. and EMFAX had an excellent run, a fortune 500 for sure. until middle school, when it went belly-up.

EMMA

Maxie looks pretty much
the way she always looked.
No weird tats or shaved head.

A few too many ear piercings.
And she's got a camera sticking
out of her pocket.

Which is a little hard-core.
Most everyone
I know uses their cell.

Hey, Maxie, I say.

There's a brief awkward moment
when we don't know whether
to hug or not. We don't.

But Polly immediately jumps up
on Maxie with the kind of joy
she usually reserves for me.

Faith watches, smiling.
She always liked Maxie.
I guess so did Polly.

Hey, Polly, says Maxie, rubbing Polly's ears the way

she loves. *Hey, Faith,* Maxie adds with a smile at
my sister.

I brush off the irritation
I'm feeling about
this lovefest.

> *Hey, Maxie, you want a cookie?* I say. *Faith baked the*
> *best oatmeal-raisin cookies.*
> *Sure,* says Maxie.

In the kitchen we both munch
Faith's cookies, still faintly warm
from the oven.

> *So, Maxie,* I say, *I don't know if you're into partying,*
> *but thought I'd warn you. Brendan heard about this*
> *thing at a kid's house. Probably a lot of drinking*
> *and stuff.*
> *That's fine,* says Maxie.

But I can tell by her face
she's not really okay with it.
Then I hear a car honking outside.

> *We can always drop you home if you . . . ,* I say, looking
> out the window at Brendan hopping out of his SUV.
> *No, it's cool,* she says, too quickly.
> I shrug. *Great,* I say.

When we get back outside,

Brendan is chatting with
Mom and Dad.

Maxie pulls out her camera and
points it toward Faith and Polly,
who are curled up together on the front stoop.

Flash.

Faith looks up and smiles,
while Polly bounds over
to Maxie again.

I can tell Brendan is impatient
to get going. So am I. I grab his hand
and pull him toward the car.

C'mon, Maxie, I call. *We gotta go. Bye Mom, bye Dad.*

Time to get this
party started. Time for
some serious fun.

MAXIE

Emma is still Emma,
only more so.

More assured,
more full of life.
Shinier.

And, I have this feeling,
even harder
to say
no to.

FAITH

I love
how Polly
knew Maxie
right away.
Dogs are
amazing.

And I'm glad
Maxie has
moved back.
Maybe she
and Emma
will be
friends again.
But probably
not.

Emma is on
her own
fast track,
the way
she's been
since
middle school.
No patience for
anyone
a little
different.

BRENDAN

Took the turn onto Elm a little wide.
A car blares its horn at me.

Emma shoots me a look. So, yeah,
I've had a few beers already. Big deal.

No DUI yet and I've driven
hammered plenty of times.

It's those Donnelly reflexes,
the ones my dad takes the credit for.

"Yeah, that's my boy, the star athlete,
just like his old man."

Fine, long as it gets me that free ride
to college somewhere far away.

Colorado or California,
that's where I'd go.

But of course the old man has
his sights set on his alma mater.

"Ivy's the way to go, boy. You'll make connections
there that'll set you up for life." Fuck that.

Want me to drive? Emma asks.

I'm cool, I say.

Okay, if you're sure, Emma says.

She picks up my iPod, searching for a song.

I turn the AC a notch higher.

So, Anil, what's your dad do? I say, catching his eye in
the rearview mirror.

He and Chloe are in the third row.

She's got her hands all over him.

He's a doctor, Anil says.

Anil's mom is a doctor, too, Chloe pipes up.

Two doctors in the family,
must be loaded.

My little brothers go to your mom, says Chloe.

They do? Anil says, his voice surprised.

Yeah, didn't I tell you?

Emma makes one of her impatient
noises, shaking my iPod.

It keeps freezing, she says.

Battery's low, I say.

Then I catch Anil's eye again

in the rearview mirror.

And he looks so superior,
I can't help myself, saying

Hey, bro, speaking of your mom. She is smoking hot.

Both his parents came out to say good-bye
when I picked up Anil and Chloe.

Shut up, Bren, says Emma.
What? I say, with innocent eyes. Just sayin' I could
totally do her.
You're so gross, Emma says, but not really paying
attention.

She's finally found the song she was
looking for and plugs the iPod back in.

Thought I might get some
kind of rise from Anil. But no.

In the rearview mirror I see he's just staring
out the window, no expression at all.

Mr. Poker Face might not be so calm if he knew
what my dad accidentally left in the glove compartment.

ANIL

1. Anger,
like nothing I've felt before,
courses through me.
Blood heats my skin,
and I want nothing more than
to punch Brendan Donnelly
in the face.

I've never hit anyone in my life,
but I know, with a mathematical certainty,
that if I weren't pinned back
in the third row of this SUV,
I would hit Brendan.
It's a physical, palpable thing
in my gut.

Chloe leans into me.

Ignore him, she whispers. *He's a jerk.*

Her breath in my ear distracts me.
But I can still feel the pulse throbbing in my neck.
My blood pressure must be sky-high.

I liked your mom, says Chloe in a soft voice.
She's nice.

2. I think back to their meeting.

My mom was shy but warm,
and my dad was easy to read.

Okay, I see now, his eyes said to me.

3. My thoughts go back to Brendan,
what he said.
Why did I react that way?
I've heard worse in the weight room.
Jocks mouthing off,
showing off.
I should be able to joke back.

Yeah, bet your mom is hot, too, I should have said.

Is it the Indian in me?
My father in me?
These disrespectful American teenagers.

But then I get a sudden image
of Brendan standing beside my mother,
putting his hands on her,
and my hands curl into fists again.
My breath goes short.

I almost feel like
I could drive my fists through the
car window beside me and
not feel a thing.

FAITH

Mom and
Dad are
watching a
movie in
the family
room.

I'm about
to join
them,
bringing
a plate of
cookies.
But just
before I
enter,
before they
can see me,
I hear
Brendan's
name.
I stand
very still,
hardly
breathing
so I can
hear them
over the TV.

I don't get why you don't like him, Dad is saying.
Brendan seems like a good kid to me, very polite.
I don't know. I guess I think it's an act, Mom answers.
And I've heard stuff about his father.
What kind of stuff?
That he makes the Great Santini look like a walk in the
park, Mom answers.

I'm dying
for her to
go on,
explain
what she
means,
but Dad
just gives a
chuckle,
like he
knows.

Still, that doesn't make him a bad kid, even if his father
is a sonofabitch, he says.

And then
the ad that
was playing
ends and
the movie
they were
watching

starts up
again.

I'm frozen
for a
moment.
I don't
think I've
ever heard
my dad
use that
word before.
And even
if I don't
know who
the Great
Santini is,
it's pretty
clear he's
bad news.
And,
truth is,
I don't
want to
feel sorry for
Brendan
Donnelly.

POLICE CHIEF AUBREY DELAFIELD

Things are starting to get busy.
As predicted.

Last night some middle school boys
rounded up a bunch of stone statues
from all over Wilmette—
geese, rabbits, even one of those old-fashioned jockeys—
and stuck them in the sand at Gillson Park beach.

Of course the tide came in,
knocking them down, dragging some of them
out into the lake.

Sorting the damn things out,
wading out to retrieve the ones
caught out on the first sandbar
and figuring out which one belonged to which address,
was a nightmare.

One lady made a great hue and cry because
the little Northwestern sweatshirt
she'd had specially made for her goose
got washed away by the tide.
And one garden gnome never did turn up.

Like I said, it's going to be a long weekend.
But if looking for a goose's sweatshirt is the worst of it,
I'll be a happy man.

MAXIE

Brendan pulls up
in front of
Felix's house.

So many memories around that house:
      epic games of freeze tag
          with flashlights.
      eating doughnuts in the big oak tree
          in the backyard.
      his mom making the best grilled cheese sandwiches
          and Campbell's tomato soup,
          with crumbled-up saltines.

The house looks
different somehow
and at first I can't put
my finger on it.

But then I realize there aren't
any lights on
in the windows.
Plus the lawn needs
mowing and tall weeds
crowd the front bushes.

It almost looks
deserted.

Felix's house is in
the part of town where
the houses are smaller
and closer together.
Felix's parents are young,
and his dad is
    in the military.

But his mom always
used to keep their house
neat and pretty.

    I heard his mom is working a couple of jobs, says
    Emma, *while his dad is in Afghanistan.*

I notice a small orange glow
near the front door
and realize someone is
sitting on the front steps,
    smoking.

Brendan lowers Emma's window
and leans over her.

    Put down the blunt, dude, he yells, *and get your butt*
        over here.
    Nice, says Emma. *That lady next door probably*
        heard you.
    So what, says Brendan.

The orange glow gets brighter

for a second,
then
goes out.

I hop out of
the car.

Hey, Felix, I call. *Long time no see.*

But he doesn't bound
toward me,
not the way he used to.
He moves slowly,
and his big grin is slower, too,
though it's just as warm.

Max, he says, and gives me a loose but lingering hug.

I can smell the weed on him,
strong.

His hair is the same curly mop,
but he's gotten
bigger and taller.
And something else about him,
other than the slower speed
and smell of pot,
is different.

I can't figure out what it is,
not right away.

It's great to see you, he says.

And he means it,
I can tell.

    Come on, calls Brendan from inside the car. *We've got
places to go.*

Brendan says we need
to make a quick
fueling stop
before we head
to the party
and I think he means
    a gas station,
but he pulls into
the parking lot
by Centennial Park, near the
    kid's playground.

    Time for some pre-party refreshments, says Brendan.

The playground is deserted.
Under the nearly
    full moon
the swing set and jungle gym
look like skeletons of
    long-ago
prehistoric creatures.

    What've you got? asks Emma.

The cooler's between you two, says Brendan to me and
    Felix. *Pop it open.*

Felix is slow to respond
so I reach down
and unlatch the cooler,
opening the lid.
    Nestled in ice
    are about a
    dozen brightly
    colored cans
    of what looks
    like soda pop.

Emma peers
into the cooler.

Holy shit, where'd you find that stuff?
Craigslist, says Brendan proudly. *Only fifteen bucks*
    a can.
What is it? I ask, amazed by how expensive those
    colorful cans are.
Don't they have MoonBuzz in Colorado? Brendan says.

I shake my head.

Then you are in for a treat, Brendan says with a
    big grin.
I heard it was banned in Illinois, comes Chloe's voice
    from the back.
Yep. That's why it was such a rip-off, says Brendan.

But believe me, it's worth it. Cocaine in a can.
I've read about it, comes Anil's voice from the back.
   They say drinking one can is the equivalent of five
   beers and a cup of Starbucks coffee.
Sweet, says Brendan.

He grabs one can
for him and one
for Emma.

   Help yourselves, he says to the rest of us.

It sounds
really
bad to me.

But Felix reaches into the cooler,
fishes out a couple
and hands them back to
   Chloe and Anil.

Then he picks out two more,
and offers one to me
   with a wink.

I start to say no,
but then
catch Emma watching me
in the rearview mirror.
So I take it,

setting it on the floor
at my feet.

Then I open
the car door.

> *I'll be right back,* I say, sliding my camera out of my
> pocket.

ANIL

1.   I watch the girl named Maxie
as she stops just short of the playground.
She holds a camera to her eye.

Flash.

Chloe has popped open her can of MoonBuzz.
I can hear her take a few gulps.
Then she says,

> *C'mon, Anil, I want to swing.*

I follow Chloe as she runs,
childlike and a little clumsy,
to the swing set.

As I pass Maxie she gives me a small,
almost embarrassed, crooked smile.

> *That'll make a nice shot,* I say, *with the moon
> and all.*
> *It reminds me of dinosaur bones,* she answers
> with a laugh.

I look over at the swing set,
where Chloe is waiting for me.

> *I see that,* I say.

And I do.
We exchange smiles again.

    Anil, Chloe calls. *Come push me.*

Chloe is wearing a white dress tonight
and flying through the air on the swing,
she looks like the goddess Lakshmi,
the Hindu embodiment of beauty,
or she would if the goddess Lakshmi
had honey-colored hair.

2.   Automatically I push Chloe,
    high and higher,
    but for some reason
    all I can think about is
    that small, embarrassed, slightly crooked
    smile on Maxie's face.

    Hey, Chloe says, *I said stop.*

And I realize that I've been pushing
while she's been trying to slow down.

    Sorry, I say.

I look over at the SUV,
thinking about the MoonBuzz
and how I do not want to drink it.

    You're not mad at me or anything? Chloe asks,

interrupting my thoughts.

Huh? I say. *Uh, no, I'm not. But, hey, Chloe, maybe*
don't drink too much of that stuff of Brendan's.
It's especially dangerous for girls, I mean,
because you're smaller.

I know. I won't, she says. *You're so sweet.*

And she slides out of the swing
and comes right up to me,
wrapping her arms around my waist,
her head nestled at my chest.

It feels good.
Sometimes I still can't believe
that Chloe Carney wants to be with me.
I put my arms around her,
but out of the corner of my eye
I catch sight of Maxie getting back
into the car.

FELIX

while the anil kid and chloe carney are off at the swing
set, probably making out, brendan's cell buzzes. he gets
out of the car to answer it. max reappears, sliding back
into her seat. she doesn't open her moonbuzz and i can
tell she doesn't want to drink it. not my favorite brew
either, but no big.

up front, emma is slowly, steadily drinking hers, quiet,
watching brendan through the front windshield. suddenly
she turns around and looks me straight in the eye.

> *Why'd you quit soccer, Felix?* Emma asks.
> *Tore my ACL,* I say.

she keeps looking at me. then shakes her head.

> *That was sophomore year. I saw you play since then,*
> *that game with Harvest Prep last year. You were*
> *amazing. A rock star.*

i was, too. got a recruiting e-mail a week later from
georgetown.

> *So?* she says.
> *Never healed right. And I reinjured it.*

she turns back to looking out the front windshield. i can
tell she doesn't believe me.

That was some game, she says. *That Harvest Prep game.*

she's right about that. some game, best i ever played. best
night of my life, until it turned into the worst night of my
life. the night my world went away. vanished. kerflooey.

Anyone want a hit? I say.

i can feel max looking at me, puzzled. she still wears how
she feels on her face, even when she's trying not to. one
of the things i always liked about her. nobody else says
anything. until emma pipes up, her voice a little fuzzy
already.

*Too bad about that ACL. Bet you would've gotten a
    full ride.*
Yeah, I say with a shrug.

would've, could've, should've.

MAXIE

Ever since he got in the car
I've been trying to figure out
Felix.
What's different about him,
other than
     the pot.

And suddenly
it hits me.

Underneath
the grin
and the nonchalance
and the smoke,
     Felix is sad.
     I mean really sad.

     Hey, douche bags, let's go, calls Brendan to Anil and
     Chloe, who are entwined by the swing set. *Axel said
     to get over there, party's starting to rock.*

I am so *not* looking forward
to this
     so-called "rocking" party.

It's not that I'm anti-drinking.
Don't mind a glass or two of wine,
getting a little tipsy

like we sometimes did
 back in Colorado.

But kids at these kinds of parties,
the kind Mr. MoonBuzz,
cocaine-in-a-can Brendan,
would want to go to,
well, we're not talking a *little* buzz.
We're talking a messy,
drink till you puke
 all over yourself
 booze fest.

And somehow it's just
not the way
I want to meet and greet
these kids I'll be seeing for
the first time
in four years.

The party house has tons of cars
parked in front and
music blaring from open windows.
Brendan has to park
a few blocks away
and just as he turns off the motor
I spot a kid
 throwing up
 into a neighbor's
 pot of geraniums.
 Nice.

Welcome back to Illinois, Max, says Felix, who saw the
guy, too.

I take a
deep breath.

As everyone begins to pile out,
Felix looks sideways at me.

> *Hey, guys,* he announces, *I'm feeling a little trashed.
> Think I'll stay here. Keep me company?* he adds in my
> direction.

I nod,
relieved.

> *Lightweight,* Brendan says but tosses Felix the car
> keys. *Lock it when you decide to come in. Just don't be
> going joyriding or anything. And guard that MoonBuzz
> with your life. If any's missing when I get back, you're
> dead meat.*

Anil and Chloe climb past us again.
I'm getting used to her
sweet, fruity perfume
and his
clean, soapy smell.

> *Thanks,* I say to Felix after they're gone. *You must be
>   a mind reader.*
> *Your face is pretty easy to read, Max.*

I know, I say. *It's really annoying.*
No, I like it. Besides, I'm not that into partying.

I look at him,
skeptical.

Well, not this kind of party. Stoner parties are a lot
mellower. Speaking of which . . .

He pulls out a plastic bag
and some papers.
I watch him expertly
    roll a joint,
    then light it.

So, Felix, how are you really? I ask.
Good, he murmurs. *Better now,* he adds, inhaling
    deeply.

He has a wide
blissy
smile
on his face.

Are you and Emma friends still? I ask.
Nah. Not since 5th grade, he says.
That's not true, I say. *The three of us would hang out*
    in middle school.
Not really, Max. I'd tag along sometimes. But she was
    gone, for me. On her way out with you, too.

I nod.
Felix is right.
I had tried to hold on, but it was
a losing battle.
I cried a lot about it.
Mom said I was too
        sensitive.

        Emma will always be your friend, she'd say.

Like I said,
clueless.

Felix passes me
the joint.
I take a very small hit.
I'm not too into pot.

        You like Brendan at all? I ask.
        Dude's a jerk, he says.
        What does Emma see in him? I say.

Felix gives me a look.

Okay, right. He's hot, I say with a grin.

And Brendan *is* hot,
I mean right-off-the-TV-screen kind of hot.
        Dimples,
        perfect nose,

tousled hair.
Six-pack
and then some.

Only the best for Emma, Felix says, but not bitter.
Bitter's not Felix's style.

I laugh.

She always had to win everything, didn't she? I say.
  Board games, races, hopscotch.
*Climb the tree the highest, swing highest, throw the ball
  farthest,* Felix says.
Get the most valentines, I say.

A pause.

It's why I was so good at soccer, Felix says,
unexpectedly.

He looks a little surprised
at what he said.

Why? I ask, curious.
*She was always after me to play, had to beat me of
  course. And I couldn't let a girl do that. Sorry,* he
  adds, *but it's a fact.*

I smile.
Then it hits me

what Felix said,
that he
    was so good at soccer,
not
    am so good at soccer.

    Seems like it bothers Emma you don't play anymore, I
say slowly.

Felix is quiet.

    *Is that really why you stopped, because you tore
your ACL?*

There's a pause.

    Then he says, *No, it's not.*

FELIX

thing is, i don't know if it was the weed (it was some strong shit). or the combination of weed and moonbuzz. or if it was seeing max after so long. but it all came pouring out.

for the first time i told someone. i told her.

about how the best day of my life turned into the worst.

mom said afghanistan changed my dad, which i didn't believe at first. seemed like too much of an excuse. but he did get angry a lot. he'd yell at my soccer games, got thrown out a few times. he was there that night we played harvest prep, nothing to yell about that night, but he did anyway.

mom dragged him away so neither of them even saw the last goal i scored, amazing shot. trapped a pass on my chest then did a bicycle kick, my back to the goal, lasered it in. i could tell i'd scored from the swell of cheering as i landed flat on my back, the wind knocked out of me. got the whole hero thing, up on the shoulders, paraded around like i was a rock star.

went to a party afterward and this girl betsy comes up to me and kisses me, just like that. right away she apologizes but then blurts out that she was tired of waiting around to see if i'd ever kiss her first. she's cute. i'd noticed her before. not emma, but nice and for the first time i'm thinking maybe it's time to give up on that old dream of emma and me 'cause it's never gonna happen. maybe i'll give it a try with betsy. hang out with her some. the kiss felt nice.

but then i come home.

it's one in the morning, and i'm feeling good, nice good, not drunk or anything, and i go up the stairs and suddenly there's this crashing sound from my parents' bedroom, then dad letting out a bunch of cuss words. i kind of freeze, standing there in the hall, and that's when the bedroom door flies open and mom is standing there and all she's wearing is a bra with a strap missing and the hall light shows her face, swollen up and some blood around her lip. but even worse, much worse, is the blood i see trickling down her leg, the inside of her thigh. then i hear dad's voice yelling *i'm your husband, you frigid bitch. husbands and wives have sex, that's what they do, and don't you fucking call it rape. that's bullshit.*

i'm getting this prickling psycho feeling all over my skin and i feel like every muscle in my body has turned into stone and i couldn't move if i wanted to. then my eyes meet mom's eyes and she lets out a little sound, a whimper, like a hurt animal, and she rushes past me to the bathroom. she shuts the door behind her and i can hear water running.

then dad comes lumbering out of the bedroom, dressed in t-shirt and jeans. he sees me. his face is red, his eyes wild. looks at me like he doesn't know me. pushes past me and runs downstairs, through the kitchen, then out to the garage. i can hear the sound of the garage door opening and the car start. i still can't move. next i know, it's backing up and he's gone.

i knew dad yelled a lot but i'd never seen him hit mom. then i remembered seeing a big purple/green bruise on her arm, that she said was from bumping into something. there was another one on her leg. she had an excuse for it, too.

finally i can move again and i go to the bathroom door.

mom?

no answer. the water's still running. maybe she's in the shower. i try again, call her. no answer again. i stand there. think about going after dad. think i might want to kill him and if i hadn't been turned to stone like i was, i would have.

finally the water stops. after a few minutes the bathroom door opens and mom comes out, wearing a robe, her hair wet, her eye still swollen shut. but she's calm. too calm.

she says, *felix, honey, i'm okay. don't worry. can i fix you a sandwich?*

i nod, numb. and it's like we're two people who barely know each other, chatting about the weather. i can tell she wants it this way, really bad. so i let her. let her make me a grilled cheese sandwich, watch her slice the cheddar cheese, watch her heat up the small blue skillet she always uses for grilled cheese sandwiches, watch her butter both sides of the bread, watch the butter sizzle when it hits the pan, and even though it's a perfect grilled cheese sandwich, oozy cheese, bread nicely browned, not burnt, i can't eat more than one bite and that one bite tastes like hot glue, burning my tongue and sticking in my throat.

i wonder later if i should have let her act that way, like nothing was wrong. if things would've been different. because the next day it was like nothing happened. except that i couldn't look at dad without wanting to hit him and then he announced at dinner that he was going back for another tour of duty. in a week. which was a month earlier than he'd said before. mom didn't say anything. just kept cutting her pot roast into smaller and smaller pieces.

after he left i tried to talk to mom. asked if she was okay. if she was going to stay with dad.

and she looked at me all in surprise, and asked why i'd say something like that. and i stammered out something about that night and how dad hurt her, and she interrupted me, saying i must have misunderstood what i saw. that dad was a hero. and she loved him.

i scored my first dime bag the next day. because i know what i saw.

i stop talking then. max looks at me like i've just vomited up a stinking mass of gopher guts, which i might as well have.

Oh, Felix, she says, her eyes all glimmery like she
might cry.

and then she puts her arm around my shoulders and
squeezes me hard and damn if i don't burst into tears like
i'm a freaking baby. but she just holds tight.

when i finally stop, she fishes in her bag and comes up
with a few tissues, which i fill up with snot.

Whoa, I say. *Sorry about that,* I add with a feeble
attempt at a grin.
You need to talk to someone, Max says.
I just did, I say.
Still, Felix. What happened . . . it's not right.
Hey listen, Max, I'm okay, I say. *I really am.*

and i light up another joint.

MAXIE

Other than saying
I'm sorry,
which seems so little,
so lame,
I am without words.

I only remember
Felix's dad as teasing,
cheerful, and young,
younger than most
of the other dads.

He played Wiffle ball with us,
and even the board game Mouse Trap,
which we were obsessed with
        for a while.

A rapist?

I take the joint Felix offers me,
take a hit,
then cough
most of it out.

Felix chuckles,
taking the
joint back.

Lightweight, he teases, imitating Brendan.

We're quiet for a moment,
listening to the loud music
coming from the
party house.

> *You leave a boyfriend back there in Colorado, Max?*
> he asks.

I blush a little.

> *No,* I say. *There was one guy I liked, but he wound up*
> *with my friend Mandy. And they're good together, better*
> *than me and him, so it was okay. How about you?*

Then I could kick myself,
remembering his story about
the girl named Betsy and
    the kiss.

But he isn't thinking about
Betsy.

> *Nah,* he says. *Too many years worshipping at the altar*
> *of Emma.*

I'd known for a long time
that Felix had a thing
for Emma,
though tonight's the first time

he's said it
out loud.

But I could always tell
from the way
his eyes would
follow her,
even back in 5th grade,
with this hopeful,
awestruck expression
when he thought
    no one
    was
    looking.

    Yeah, well, just for the record, you're a million times
        better than any Brendan.
    Which isn't saying a whole lot, Felix laughs. *Since I*
        can tell you like Brendan about as much as that can
        of MoonBuzz.
    No kidding, I say.

Abruptly I open the car door wide,
grab the MoonBuzz can by my seat,
and turn it upside down.
Then watch, as bright red-pink liquid
gushes out,
into the gutter.

ANIL

1. I leave the party by a kitchen door,
   hoping no one notices me go,
   and also hoping maybe Felix and Maxie
   are still in Brendan's car.

   Feeling jittery, unhappy.
   An outside observer would probably think it was
   because I saw Chloe's old boyfriend, Josh,
   coming on to her.

   But they'd be wrong.

   Yes, I saw Josh put his hand on her waist
   in that casual, I've-had-sex-with-you way,
   but what surprised me most about it was
   how much it *didn't* bother me.

   What did
   was the smile she flashed at him.
   It was exactly the same smile
   she gave me when I walked up with a cup of punch.
   And, in fact, the same smile
   she gave Emma and Brendan
   when they joined us.

   Don't get me wrong.
   It's a good smile. A winning smile.
   The kind you see in glossy magazines.

But,
I keep thinking about Maxie,
her seeing a swing set as dinosaur bones.
And her smile,
that small, crooked smile,
a real smile,
that Chloe Carney's lips,
no matter how perfect,
can never replicate.

2. Smoke is drifting out of an
open window of the SUV.
So I know at least Felix is still in there.

He should probably be more careful.
Chloe said the neighbors on both sides
are at vacation homes in Wisconsin,
but this is the kind of party
that'll eventually get busted.

Which makes me ready to get out of here.
My dad would kill me if I got picked up
by the police the weekend before school starts.

3. I come up to the window
and Felix spots me.

   Dude, he says. *Join us.*

So I do, sitting on the backseat floor,
my legs sticking out the open car door,

declining the joint Felix offers.

How's the party? he asks.
Pretty crazy, I say.

I sneak a look at Maxie, who is leaning back
in her seat, eyes closed.
The lavender shirt she's wearing
looks nice on her.

Whoa, says Felix, *I think I just saw a comet or
shooting star or something.*

Felix's eyes, which are trained upward
through the glass moonroof, are very red.
Must be pretty far gone on weed.

Sure, Felix, Maxie says.

But she opens her eyes
and follows his gaze upward
through the moonroof.

Then she looks back at Felix
with a tender expression on her face,
like she really cares about this guy.

I wonder if they're dating
and feel this weird stab of jealousy.

What the hell, I think to myself.

I barely know this girl.
And I have a girlfriend. Chloe Carney.

> *No, really,* says Felix. *I swear something streaked*
> *across the sky.*
> *I once saw a comet,* I say.
> *Really?* says Maxie.

4. So I find myself telling about the time
when I was a kid
and my dad got two telescopes.
He'd heard about the McNaught comet
that was due to show the brightest
on January 12 that year.
Two telescopes so Dad and I could watch
at the same time.

And I remember putting my eye
up to the telescope, feeling the cold metal
circling my eye socket.
I looked up at the midnight blue of the sky,
dotted with all those radiant specks of white,
spread out randomly as if someone had
carelessly strewn fistfuls of diamonds
onto a black cloth.

I saw it, that McNaught comet,
a thin stream of light across the night sky.

> *This is a very historic moment, Anil,* my dad said,
> his voice solemn.

The brightest comet in thirty years,
he told me,
and it would probably be that long, or longer,
before another one as bright came along.

And I find myself telling Maxie and Felix
that at age ten I suddenly got freaked out,
realizing that the next time
a big comet came along
my dad would be an old man,
maybe even dead.
And I might even be a father myself.

I remember feeling terrified,
like my life was this speeding train
you can't stop.

I shut up then, embarrassed that I'd said
all that stuff.

Dude, says Felix. *You're messing me up.*

5. Felix starts rolling a new joint.
Maxie is quiet though.
I can tell she's thinking about what I said,
really thinking about it.

Yeah, she finally says. *I know what you mean.*

There is a pause,
and then she goes on.

But sometimes the opposite is true. Sometimes it
slows down. Little moments. Like now, she adds
suddenly, with a sweet smile that for some reason
tugs at my heart.

Felix lights the new joint
and takes a deep pull on it.
Breathes out a cloud of smoke.

I can't take my eyes off of Maxie's face,
through the smoky haze inside the SUV.
And I wonder if I'm maybe getting a secondhand high
off Felix's reefer.

I once had a moment like that, with my dad.
A slowed-down moment, that is, Maxie says
dreamily. *It was one summer at the beach, Gillsons*
Beach, and we found some sea glass . . .

I watch her intently,
her eyes looking back in time
at herself and her dad
on that beach.

Two pieces of sea glass. It was amazing enough to
find one, but two was something else. One was a
frosty light blue and the other was green. And my
dad got the idea that we should build a sandcastle
and use the sea glass as windows. So we set to
work, and that afternoon seemed to go on and on
as we worked on the castle under the hot sun, the

sound of waves breaking, close but not too close. I
loved it. And when we set those two pieces of sea
glass in for windows, it was perfect.

6. No one says anything for a few moments.
Maxie is still back on the beach with her dad,
and Felix has his eyes closed,
a smile on his face.

> *I like that story,* he says. *Ya know, I think that's*
> *why I like weed. It slows stuff down,* he adds.

He takes a long drag on his joint.

> *So, d'you think Brendan has anything else in this*
> *cooler besides MoonBuzz?* Maxie asks. *I'm really*
> *thirsty for water, or at least something that isn't*
> *going to kill me.*
> *Let's check it out,* says Felix.

He reaches over to open the cooler
and accidentally
he knocks his half-full can
of MoonBuzz out of the cup holder
onto Maxie,
splashing her lavender shirt
with lurid Hawaiian Punch—colored red liquid.

> *Oh shit, I'm so sorry!* Felix says.

Maxie grabs up a few used, rumpled tissues

and dabs at her shirt, but it doesn't do much good.

I look around to see if there's something,
like paper towels or rags.
Nothing.

I pop open the storage compartment
in the center console. Nothing there either.

7.   I reach over and punch the button
      on the glove compartment
      and it drops open, with a muffled thud.

      In the glow from the interior light
      I see it,
      gleaming black, just sitting there,
      filling up the glove compartment.

      A gun.

      Maxie has seen it, too,
      because she lets out a cry,
      one of astonishment and
      fear.

            What? asks Felix.

      Maxie points
      and Felix leans forward, following her gesture.

            Holy crap, Felix says, his voice a whisper.

MAXIE

My heart is pounding.

I
hate
guns.

A kid in Colorado once
showed me his dad's
shotgun
and I remember staring at it and
breathing in
>the metallic,
>harsh,
>gunpowdery smell.

I felt cold, clammy,
like I might
>pass out.

I wouldn't touch that shotgun,
even when they
made fun
of me.

Anil reaches out
and closes
the glove compartment

with a decisive
smack.

> *Why would Brendan have a gun in his glove*
>   *compartment?* I blurt out.
> *Could be his dad's,* says Felix. *I think he's a big*
>   *pro-NRA kind of guy.*

I look down at my shirt,
splotched with MoonBuzz
red.
Like I've been shot.
      I shiver.

I am having
a really
bad feeling
about this whole evening.

> *You okay, Max?* Felix asks.
> *Okay,* I say, my voice sounding thin, even to me.
> *I gotta take a leak,* Felix says. *And while I'm in there,*
>   he adds, rubbing his eyes, *I'll find Brendan and tell*
>   *him some of us want to get out of here.*
> *Thanks, Felix,* I say.

Anil settles himself back
on the floor of the SUV,
his long legs
sticking out the door again.

It's too bad about your shirt, he says. *It's nice. Looks really good on you.*

And even though it's
pretty dark
in the car,
I can clearly see he's
blushing.

> *Wow, that sounded lame, didn't it,* he says.
> *Sorta,* I say, trying not to smile. *But thanks.*

We laugh, awkwardly,
and then he
suddenly flashes me
his own smile.
>   Heart-stopping.

Okay.
So now I get why
Chloe Carney is with him.
Which makes me want to go home
even more,
though at the very same time
I don't want
to go
>   at all.

To cover my confusion,
I take out
my camera,

pretending like I'm making sure
it didn't get any
MoonBuzz on it.

> *You like to take pictures?* Anil asks.
> *I do,* I say. *I'm on the wait list for Mrs. Pawley's
>   photography class.*
> *Yeah, she's good. What about working for the school
>   paper?* he asks.

I nod,
pressing the power button of
the camera
on and then off.

> *Was thinking I'd try for it, either that or the literary
>   magazine. What's it called,* <u>Versions</u> *or something?*
> *Yeah, think you'd probably like that better, better than
>   the paper I mean.*
> *Why?*
> *You'd be doing more creative stuff, not so many lacrosse
>   games. Plus I'm the editor of the paper, and people
>   say I'm a pain to work for.*

That smile again.

> *Though we sure could use a good photographer,* he says.

Between that and the shirt comment
I'm wondering if Anil could actually be
flirting with me,

even though he doesn't seem like the
flirting type.

There you are, comes Emma's voice. *Chloe's been
looking all over for you.*

Anil stands up,
looking guilty.

Where's Felix? Brendan says, hopping into the driver's
seat. *Jesus, my car smells like freaking Lollapalooza.*

He powers down
all the windows.

Party's lame, Brendan says. *Emma wants to grab a
burger or something.*

As he puts the key
in the ignition,
Felix appears,
with Chloe close behind him.

When she and Anil slide past me
I get this strange, light-headed feeling
breathing in
his soapy smell.

Between the MoonBuzz
and whatever else they had at the party,

both Emma and Chloe are
pretty drunk.

Not gross drunk,
just giggly on Chloe's part
and loud on Emma's.

I find myself trying to
block out
Chloe's throaty little giggles
coming from
  behind me.

CHLOE

"Who You Should Fall in Love with, According to My Mom"

I'm a little messed up.

I think Anil saw Josh coming on to me.
He's such a jerk,
Josh I mean.

      Who wants something? says Brendan.

He's pulled into a drive-through
fast-food place.

A milk shake suddenly sounds amazing.
Anil gets one, too,
and he pays,
so maybe he's not too mad at me.

Toward the end with Josh,
he stopped paying for stuff for me.
Said it was because he lost
his job at the gas station.
But I wondered.

I can't remember what Josh did exactly,
at the party,
maybe put his hand on my ass.
But I know Anil saw.

When Josh and I first got together,
sophomore year,
he was so devoted.

But middle of junior year
he started slipping away.
I could feel it.
Like he was distracted.
Bored even.
It sucked, and I didn't know how to
stop the slide.

No matter how cute I looked,
how much I smiled.

Then it came,

> *Sorry, babe.*
> *This just isn't working out.*
> *Hope we can stay friends.*

Yeah, friends with benefits.
I don't think so.

So I looked around.
And not that I want to brag
but there always seem to be guys
who want to be with me.

But no one else did anything for me,
not like Josh.

Till I saw Anil on the tennis court.
He was hot.
Plus he's, what's the right word,
decent.
Nice.

Nice.
For some reason that word
makes me giggle.
I know I'm giggling too much.

> *How's the milk shake?* Anil asks.
> *Cold. Creamy,* I say.

I giggle again.
Stop it, I tell myself.

> *How come you never told me your brothers go to my*
>   *mom?* Anil suddenly asks.
> *Dunno,* I say back. *It's not a big deal, is it?*
> *No,* he says. *Except it seems sort of weird I didn't even*
>   *know you had brothers.*

And it *is* weird,
weird that I've never brought Anil home.

But here's why:
        my mom would see this good-looking Indian guy
        with a 4.0 and his two doctor parents
        and she'd be like,
        oh my god,

all drooly over him,
because if she's said it once
she's said it a thousand times:
Chloe honey, it's just as easy to fall in love
with a future doctor
as it is to fall in love
with a future garage mechanic.

And I really don't *ever* want Anil
to see that look
in my mom's eyes.

FAITH

Mom and
Dad are in
the kitchen,
cleaning up.
Polly is
curled
at the
foot of
my bed.

I'm looking
at an old
photo album,
thinking
about Emma.
About Emma
before
Brendan.

Emma
always
had boys
liking her.
Always.
But she
never wanted
a boyfriend.

Not until
Brendan.
Sometimes
I think
she just
thought she
should try
it, the way
she likes
to try
everything,
at least
once.

Right away
I didn't
like him,
even though
he looked
like a
fairy-tale
prince,
with his
blond curls
and dimples.

At first
I thought
it was
because he
took up

so much of
Emma's time,
that I was
jealous.
And I guess
that was
part of it.
Truth is,
I've barely
seen Emma
this summer.

Not like last
summer.
We actually
hung out
a fair amount
then.

In fact,
my very
favorite
Emma
memory
was that
July.

Mom and Dad
were away,
at a
conference

for lawyers
in New Orleans.

Emma
and I were
watching TV,
reruns of
a silly show
about rich kids
living in
New York.

We hadn't
even noticed
it was
raining
when suddenly
beeps
and warnings
came on
the TV.

Severe
thunderstorms
heading toward
Cook County.
The little
fluorescent
map in
the corner
of the screen

flashing
urgently.

Suddenly
we heard
the roaring
sound of
high winds
and lashings
of rain
on the
window.

And just
like that,
the lights
flickered
and went
out.

Awesome, said Emma.

We scouted
around for
flashlights,
found none
that worked.

By the time
we got

candles lit,
the storm
had blown
through.
A quick,
vicious hit
that left
the power
out for
days.

Freezers
full of:

    melting Popsicles,
    thawed T-bone steaks
    and mushy boxes of Lean Cuisine.

While we were
looking
for candles,
Emma found
our old
dress-up
trunk.

    C'mere, Faith, she called down the hall to me.

And in the
candlelight
we opened up

the trunk
and all
kinds of
memories
came
crowding out.

We each picked
a favorite gown.
Mine was
an old
wedding dress
of our
Aunt June's.
It's a hippie
wedding dress
with a
high neck
and delicate
ivory lace.

Emma picked
a deep purple
ball gown
of Mom's,
from her
sorority days,
which shows
a lot of
cleavage.
Then Emma

grabbed
my hand
and we
ran out
into the
backyard,
which was
covered with
wet leaves
and branches,
like nature
had been
having
a big old
crazy party
and left
a serious mess
behind.

But then it was
peaceful
and bright,
the yellow
half-moon
perched on
top of a
puffy bank
of silvery
clouds.
Emma led
me over

to the old
hammock,
soggy with rain,
and we both
lay back
onto it
side by side,
the way
we always
used to
when we
were younger.

We rocked
ourselves,
pushing
the ground
with our feet,
and looking
up at the
yellow moon.

Then Emma
took the
old lace
from my dress
between
her fingers.

You ever think about getting married, Faith? she asked.
No, I said.

She rolled
sideways on
the hammock
and looked
at me,
her head
propped on
her hand,
her elbow
sticking through
the mesh
of the
hammock.

Why not? she asked.

And finally
for the
first time,
I came
right out
and said it.

I don't like boys.

I held
my breath.

That's okay, said Emma. *You've got plenty of time
  for that.*
Yeah, I said. *Thing is, I think I like girls.*

She knew what
I meant.
I could tell
by the
flicker in
her eyes.
And I
expected,
Ew, Faith,
really?
But she
surprised me.
Sometimes
Emma
does that.

Well, that's okay, too, she said.

Then she
reached over
to take
my hand,
giving it
a good
warm
squeeze.

And in that
moment,
in that
one little

squeeze,
I felt a
big weight
slide off
my heart.

    Thanks, Emma, I whispered.
    Hey, Faith, Emma said abruptly, turning to look at
      me again.
    Yeah? I said.
    You're beautiful, you know. And smart. Really smart.
    Me? I was taken aback.
    Yes. More than me. Which is okay.

Emma saying
it's okay that
anyone
is *more*
anything
than her,
well, that was
a moment
to freeze
in time.

    Thanks, I said again.

Emma settled
onto her back,
looking up
at the sky.

*Oh, and I wouldn't give up on the whole marriage
thing,* she said. *By the time you're ready, I'm thinking
maybe it won't matter so much anymore who you
marry, long as you love 'em.*

And then
she suddenly
jumped up,
off the
hammock,
laughing,
and pulled
me off, too.

*C'mon, Miss Bridezilla, let's go see if we can find some
batteries and get that transistor radio to work.*

I followed
her in,
smiling at
the crisscross
pattern
of the wet
hammock
on the back
of her
purple gown.
The memory
of that night
makes me
smile.

And
I think
about
how much
I love
my big sister
and her
uncanny
way of
surprising me.
Out-of-the-
blue stuff,
sometimes
bad,
but sometimes
very, very
good.

MAXIE

We're driving around aimlessly,
eating fries,
drinking milk shakes.

> *How about we go to that new 3-D slasher movie,*
>   Brendan says. *Body parts flying at you and shit.*
> *Cool!* says Emma.
> *Ew,* giggles Chloe.
> *I'm broke,* says Felix.

I don't say anything.

Emma turns around
and stares
at me.
Then leans her head back
and laughs.

> *Holy crap, Maxie,* she says loudly, *I just remembered*
> *how freaking terrified you were of scary movies.*
> *Remember that sleepover in 4th grade when you hid in*
> *the closet and wouldn't come out and your mom had to*
> *come pick you up?*

Like I could forget.
But, hey, thanks, Emma,
    for the reminder.

Yeah, I've never been big on blood and guts, I say,
trying to sound like I think it's all one big joke. *Rules
out med school anyway.*

Lame, I know.
But Anil laughs.

Something scary sounds good, says Emma.

Brendan pops open another
MoonBuzz.

Scaring Emma sounds like my kind of challenge,
he says.

Great, I think,
remembering with a shudder
what's sitting in
 the glove
 compartment.

BRENDAN

What about you, Bren? Emma says. *Is there anything
you're scared of?*

And guess what's the first thing
that comes into my head.

My dad. Which is bullshit,
because I'm not. Not really.

He hasn't hit me since I
started working out.

Though I can't lie, his words sometimes
do a pretty good job.

But I start talking about a double black diamond
ski run I made once in Colorado.

It was awesome.
Closest I came to dying.

> *Where was it?* asks Emma's friend Maxie.
> *Mary Jane Mountain,* I start saying, *up in Winter—*
> *That's where I learned to ski, in Winter Park!* she
>   interrupts, her face all lit up. *I loved it there.*
> *I loved it there, too,* I say, remembering. *Felt like I was
>   on the top of the fucking world. Never felt so free . . .*

And I did, too. Haven't felt
that way since.

It was the next day, on the
same run, that I broke my leg.

Dad was pissed as hell.
But it was so worth it.

> *Bren?* asks Emma.
> *Sorry, just remembering that wipeout. Epic. Anyway, it's*
> *you we want to scare, right?*
> *Right.* She grins back at me.
> *What about a little game of chicken on the railroad*
> *tracks?* I say.
> *Not funny,* she says, losing the grin.

She's still pissed about what happened
earlier this summer.

I guess I did push it
a little far.

> *Okay, okay. I'm sure I can come up with something*
> *better,* I say.

MAXIE

For just a second there,
I found myself actually
liking Brendan.
When he was talking about skiing
    Mary Jane.

But now I keep my eyes
straight ahead,
while he jokes about ways to
scare Emma.

Trying not to think about
that gun
and why he would have it in his
    glove compartment.

    I know. Let's go ghosting, Chloe suddenly pipes up
    from the backseat.

There's a brief silence.
Then Brendan turns around
to look at her.

    That's so hyphy of you, Chloe, he says, with a smirk.
    What's hyphy? asks Anil.
    Nothing, says Emma. *Just Brendan showing how*
        gangsta he is.

Yeah, let's go ghostridin' the whip, Brendan says.

His smirk has turned into a laugh,
but now I can tell
that at least this time
he's laughing at himself,
a white-bread lacrosse player
pretending to be
> California hip-hop.

> *And what's that?* asks Anil.
> *Don't encourage him,* says Emma.
> *Think we need a little demonstration,* says Brendan.
> *Brendan, don't you dare . . . ,* says Emma.

Ignoring her,
he slows the car down.

> *So you put the car in drive,* Brendan says, *and then you
> do this . . .*

And he opens his door,
and suddenly jumps out of
the moving car,
doing these
herky-jerky dance moves
next to the car as it
> rolls forward.

> *Get the hell back in the car,* shouts Emma.

She leans over, grabbing
the steering wheel.

He ignores her
and then
jumps up
on the hood.

> *Shit,* says Emma, moving sideways into the driver's
> seat.

She steps on the brake slowly
so Brendan won't be
thrown off,
but he slides backward anyway,
almost to the end of the hood.
But then he wriggles back up,
smooshing his face up
against the windshield
with a maniacal
grin.

> *Stop it, Bren,* Emma yells, opening the car door wide.

And he slides off the hood
and jumps back
in the car,
shoving Emma into the
passenger seat.

> *You're such a dick,* she says, pushing back.

Brendan just laughs.

You guys, I meant ghosting, as in looking for ghosts,
calls Chloe from the backseat.

So she wasn't talking about the
ghosting I remember
from when I was a little girl.
the one with
Tootsie Rolls
and running away,
     giggling.

Like in a cemetery or something, Chloe adds, putting
on some fresh lip gloss.

Emma twists around
with a big
    smile.

Great idea! That's the kind of scary shit I love.
I know you do, says Chloe.

Emma glances at me
and even though I'm trying
to keep my face
blank,
I'm sure she can read me.
Like everybody
    always
      can.

Unless it's too scary for you, Maxie, Emma says.
It's cool, I say, *long as there aren't any flying body parts.*

Anil laughs again.
Either he's an easy laugh,
or he's nervous,

    like I'm nervous.

> *Where could we go?* Emma says. *The cemetery on Elm,*
>   *maybe.*
> *Has anyone here ever seen a ghost?* asks Chloe.
> *Wait, I know!* says Emma. *What about that house way*
>   *up on the north side, near the big cemetery, the one on*
>   *McKinley Road?*

No one says
anything.

> *Come on, you know,* says Emma, impatient. *Kids call*
>   *it the "ghost house" because it's all run-down and*
>   *overgrown.*
> *Oh yeah,* says Chloe.
> *Perfect,* says Brendan.

And he turns the car around.

ANIL

1.   When Chloe said ghosting,
first thing I thought about
was when you get a double image
on a TV screen
because of distortion
or multipath image signal.

That's how much of a nerd I am.

Not much of a believer in
paranormal stuff.

But I am a believer in karma.

And the moment Brendan
jumped out of the car
and did that crazy dance
I got a bad feeling.

Bad karma.

FAITH

I'm in my
bedroom,
reading.
Polly is
restless.
Wants to
go out.
Wants to
go in.

Mom and
Dad are
in the
kitchen.
I can
hear them.
Fighting.
Voices loud,
then louder.

I creep
out to
the top
of the stairs,
and perch
there,
quiet and
still, listening.

You're too soft, Mom says.
You're too rigid, Dad says.
Emma runs this house.
Let her have her fun.
We're the parents.
They're only young once.

Suddenly
quiet.
Then,
a sob in
Mom's voice.

If I have to, I'll leave. I'll take the girls and leave.

A door
slams.

ANIL

1. Chloe lays her hand on my belt buckle,
   starts fiddling, like she wants to
   unbuckle it.

   I brush her hand away.
   She giggles.

   And it's almost like one of those
   enchantment tales.
   The fairy dust falls away
   from your eyes
   and you see the frog as a prince,
   or prince as a frog.
   In this case, princess.

   Chloe Carney,
   just as beautiful as she was
   three hours ago,
   her hair the same gleaming honey color,
   her smile sweet,
   her blue eyes just as bright.

   But something between us
   has evaporated.
   like that crystal-growing science experiment
   I did as a kid.
   Except what was
   left behind then

was something beautiful—
translucent, multifaceted crystals.

What's left behind here isn't
beautiful or ugly.
It's just gone.

And not because
I'm seeing her drunk,
or because of her giggles.

And it's not even gone on account of
that smile of Maxie's.
(At least I don't think so.)

I just know I don't belong here,
with Chloe, with her friends.

2. The problem is,
    I don't want to make her sad,
    disappoint her.

    Still,
    we don't fit anymore,
    we probably never did.
    And I think she knows it, too.

MAXIE

Brendan takes a turn too fast.
My head jerks
off the headrest.

Jesus, Bren, says Emma.

Felix's eyes blink open.
Could he actually have been
asleep?
He closes them again.

I wish I were anywhere
       but here.

From behind me
I can hear Chloe giggling,
then Anil's voice,
soft,
like he's deliberately trying
not to be overheard.

Well, sor-ry, comes Chloe's voice, loud and annoying.

She leans forward,
tapping my shoulder.

Any more MoonBuzz?

Obedient,
I open
the cooler.

Me, too, says Emma.

I hand them both a colorful can,
looking down at my
ruined shirt.

Why can't I just say
I want to go home?

Is it because deep down
I actually care
what these girls think of me?
Especially Emma?
Like it would be some kind of
social suicide
to break up the party?
Pathetic.

I wasn't like that in Colorado.
It's being back here,
the new/old thing.

Just get me through tonight,
I breathe,
clenching
and

unclenching
　　my hands.

So has *anyone ever seen a real ghost?* asks Chloe again
since no one ever answered when she asked before.

She's still leaning forward,
away from Anil,
sipping her
MoonBuzz.

　　I wish, says Emma.
　　Remember how we used to do that Mary Worth thing?
　　　　asks Chloe.

I do.
At Emma's.
In 6th grade.
One of the last sleepovers we ever had,
　　just the two of us.
Scared the living shit
out of me.

In the bathroom,
lights out,
except for a single candle
perched on the toilet seat.
Looking in the mirror.

　　Just say it over and over, and you'll see her. I swear,
　　Emma said.

Except I didn't
want
to see her,
whoever she was,
this malignant white-haired
witch
named
Mary Worth.

Who,
according to Emma,
might reach out
and tear at my face
because she herself
had been
disfigured
by a bottle-wielding psycho,
the skin on her face
cut to
ribbons.

The rose-colored towels
that were hanging on the shiny chrome rack,
were transformed into
shrouds,
the shower curtain,
an undulating specter
in the candlelight.

Say it, Maxie, commanded Emma.
Mary Worth Mary Worth Mary Worth Mary Worth.

Heart pounding,
my tongue thick
    in my mouth.

The image of my face
in the mirror
suddenly went jagged,
like the glass was
    shattering.

Someone screamed.
    Me?
    Emma?

I ran out of the bathroom,
my heart
exploding
in my chest.

        Scaredy-cat! Scaredy-cat!

Hating the sound
of Emma's laughter
in my ears.

And now I wonder:
is it that
long-ago laughter
that keeps me pinned
to this leather car seat?

EMMA

I've known about the ghost house
forever.
Always wanted to check it out.

Lots of rumors.
Like someone killed someone there
back in the sixties.

Or that a bride, jilted on her
wedding day, lay dead and moldering,
still wearing her worm-infested Vera Wang gown.

Or just that a crazy old lady
lives there with her grandson,
who no one has seen in years.

Brendan is driving too fast.
Probably too drunk to be driving.
I'll drive us home.

Slow down, Bren, I say. *It's around here somewhere.*

We pass Walnut Creek Cemetery.
But I can't see any sign
of a scary-looking house.

Brendan turns around,

then parks in front of the gates
to the cemetery.

Now what? he asks.

I get out my cell, and dial my friend
Eve because she's pretty much the expert
on everything weird in this town.

FAITH

My cell phone
is ringing.
It's Emma.

    Hello? I say, eager.

How
amazing
is it that
she's
calling me
just when
I've been
thinking so
hard about
her,
wanting
to call,
but not
wanting to
make her
mad.

    Hey, Eve, this is Emma, she says. *Listen, can you tell me*
    where that ghost house is?

Eve?
For a second

I'm confused,
then realize
Emma must've
dialed wrong.
She didn't
mean to
call me
at all.

> *Emma, it's Faith,* I start.
> *Oh shit, sorry little sis. I meant to call Eve. Oh, I see,*
>   *her name's right before yours. Sorry. See ya later.*
> *Emma,* I say, urgent, *don't hang up. Mom and Dad*
>   *had this big fight and . . .*

But she's
gone.
And I
get this
prickly,
scared
feeling.

The ghost house.

And
Emma
sounded
slurry.
Off.
Drunk.

Mom: *I'll take the girls and leave.*

I won't
let that
happen.

I need
to find
Emma.
Warn her.
Don't
screw up
tonight.
It's too
important.

I know
the ghost house.
I know
how to
get there.

MAXIE

While Emma's on the phone,
I gaze out at the
graves
behind the low stone wall
of the cemetery,
rows and rows
of them,
like waves on a
>gray,
>slow-moving
>sea.

There's one streetlight
on the block
and it shines on
a statue
perched above a headstone,
almost like
>a spotlight.

>*Hold on,* I say to no one in particular. *I'll be*
>*right back.*

I open the car door,
take out my camera,
hop out into the
warm night.

It's a stone angel,
with a flowing gown
and wings.
  But no head.

Crouching, I find
the headless angel
in my viewfinder.

Flash.

WALTER

Tonight I watched *Gunfight at the O.K. Corral.*
    I watch it a lot, and Mother likes to tease me.
She says if I'd been born back in the Old West
    I'd have been one of those sheriffs.

Like Wyatt Earp
    or the marshal of Hadleyville in *High Noon,*
who faces down lawless gunslingers all by himself
    because it's his duty.

I like it when Mother kids me about that,
    because secretly I know she's right.
I would be a good sheriff
    for one of those old western towns.

I'd ride patrol on the dusty streets.
    Silver star on my chest,
leather holster with a gun on my hip,
    rifle slung across my back.

I've loved cowboys since I was a kid.
    Mother even got me cowboy bedsheets.
I slept on them until they fell apart,
    and Mother turned them into rags.

I saw her using one of those rags the other day,
    polishing the leaves of some roses she'd cut

to put in the old milky white glass vase
    with the crack in it.

Tonight I'm wearing a T-shirt Mother found for me
    at a thrift store.
It says ROCK, PAPER, SCISSORS, GUN, I WIN!
    and it's my favorite.

At first Mother didn't want to get a gun,
    but there were too many times
we could hear people in our yard, bad guys,
    so she went out and bought one. To protect us.

I'm lying in bed, wishing those old cowboy sheets
    hadn't worn out,
when a faint light flashes outside.
    It's almost like faraway lightning.

But the weatherman didn't forecast
    thunderstorms tonight.
I don't like storms.
    Neither does Mother.

I cross to my bedroom window and
    look down the block at Walnut Creek Cemetery.
And I wonder, like I always do,
    how many gunslingers are buried there.

EMMA

What's Maxie doing? I ask.
Communing with the poor dead fucks who live here.
   Brendan laughs.

I watch Maxie take pictures
of graves. Then look down at my cell
at the directions Eve texted me.

   The ghost house is about a block north of the cemetery
   entrance, I say.

Brendan polishes off his can of MoonBuzz
and crumples the aluminum in his hand,
tossing it at my feet.

   C'mon, Maxie, I call out the window, and she
      suddenly appears, climbing back in the car.
   North is the other way, I say to Brendan, impatient.
   I know, he says, with a frown.

He swings the car into
a sharp U-turn,
tires skidding.

   Go slow, I say.

And as he pulls closer, I see it, or what must be it.

An overgrown mess of shrubbery and trees,
on a corner.

There's no streetlight on this block, but the
moon is more than half full and through the foliage
I see the outline of a house. The ghost house.

FELIX

back when we were kids, when we were EMFAX, emma
was always the one who loved the thrill, the close call.
always braver than me, bolder. but i never let on when
i was scared. boys can't. and while i was reading, and
rereading, joey pigza books, emma read those goosebumps
books. one after the other.

it suddenly hits me, as i watch her lean toward brendan,
pointing through the windshield at something, that he,
brendan, is now her thrill, her close call.

i think about lighting up another joint, but i'm already too
wasted. i remember that gun in the glove compartment.
maybe i should let my head clear.

EMMA

You can hardly see the house.
It's completely dark, a dim silhouette
behind the tangle of bushes and weeds.

Like a fairy-tale castle with everyone
asleep inside. Hushed and expectant.
Waiting to be awakened.

My heart starts beating faster.
Maybe there is no crazy old lady.
Maybe it really is haunted.

I've always wanted to meet up
with something not of this world.
I mean truly.

Vampire stories, that old Mary Worth thing,
and the tales told at camp about vanishing hitchhikers
and bloody hooks dangling from car doors.

Even Santa. The tooth fairy. Easter bunny.
I always knew they were fakes.
And it pissed me off.

But a ghost. What a rush that would be,
to see something from another world,
something that most people never get to see.

ANIL

1. If my father lived next door
    to the house
    we've stopped in front of,
    with the wild, unkempt yard,
    he'd be on the phone,
    on a daily basis,
    to a local government official,
    complaining about standards
    and property values
    and respecting your neighbors.

2. From the little you can see of it
    the house looks abandoned,
    like no one has lived there
    for a long time.

    Maybe the owners moved away,
    a divorce, a job transfer,
    or an unexpected death.

    I get the sudden image in my head
    of a dead person, a corpse, lying inside,
    on a tattered rug, rotting.

3. My father once took Viraj and me
    to a master class on anatomy
    at the hospital
    to see a cadaver being cut up.

Viraj couldn't wait.
I didn't even make it into the room.
In the hallway outside, my dad started explaining
how they preserve the bodies
by pumping the arteries full of a combination of
alcohol, glycerin, and something called formalin,
which keeps the body from decomposing
from the inside out.

I barely made it to the men's bathroom,
where I threw up in a urinal.

Viraj mocked me for weeks.

4.   While I'm watching that dark, lonely house,
I suddenly see
a dim light flicker on
in a second-story window.

I see the outline of a person.
Standing there.
Looking down at us.

MAXIE

Emma turns around
and looks at the
    four of us.

I keep my eyes down,
reviewing the images of the
headless stone angel
on my camera.

    So who's coming with me? says Emma.

Brendan turns off the engine,
and the quiet in the car
suddenly seems suffocating,
like everyone has stopped
breathing at once.

I glance at Felix.
His eyes are closed again.
And I suddenly get this crazy picture
of our three younger selves,
back when we were
    EMFAX.

It's like stuff we did
in the old days.
Of course it was always

Emma who'd
dare us.

And, breathless with fear, we'd sneak up to:
      the crumbling gravestone
      the sleeping pit bull
      the house with the crabby cat-lady
      the dead chipmunk with its belly gaping open.

Urging each other onward,
a daring, heart-stopping
      adventure.

Like Jem, Scout, and Dill
in *To Kill A Mockingbird.*
A dare, to sneak a look
through the window
with the hanging shutter,
into Boo Radley's
run-down, lonely house.

And Jem does it,
but a gun goes off
and he loses
his pants.

A gun.

I start to
shiver.

Let's not, I say, so loud you can hear the shake in it.
Scaredy-cat, says Emma.

Like that long-ago sleepover,
and the words that
stung.

C'mon, Bren. Emma turns to him, laying a hand on
his arm.

He laughs.

*Hell no. I'm the getaway driver. 'Sides, I've gotta
answer this.*

He has his cell out,
texting.

Emma turns and looks back
at the rest of us again.

Who's coming? she repeats.

And her will is so strong,
like iron,
unbreakable.
I picture Felix opening his eyes
and following Emma
wherever she beckons,
         down the path,

onto the field,
along the railroad tracks,
just like he did
when we were kids.

I pray for his eyes to stay closed.
They do.
And even if it's just because he's
too stoned
I'm glad.

I glance back at Anil and Chloe.
She looks glazed.
He's staring
out the window.
Then she turns to him.

C'mon, Anil, let's go, she says, voice sweet and low.

He shakes
his head,
definite,
but with
no expression
on his face.

Fine, she says with a frown and lurches past me
and Felix.

Her perfume is overlaid

with the scent of
MoonBuzz.

Emma laughs a
happy laugh
and the two girls stand by the car,
swaying slightly and
looking up
 at the house.

 It's real dark, I hear Chloe say.

Emma snatches her cell
out of her pocket
and opens it up.

 See, just like a flashlight, she says.

Then Chloe opens up her cell, too.
I grab
my camera.
Can't resist the image of their two faces
lit up by the
 glowing
 cell phones.

Flash.

But the lighting is wrong
so I try it again without the flash

and it's
perfect.

The greenish light from their cells
makes their faces glow in an
        unearthly way.

Felix opens his eyes
at the second click of
my camera,
then closes them again.

A feeling of dread
suddenly squeezes
my heart
and I lean out the open
car door.

        Emma, don't, I call.

She ignores me.

And the two of them
begin to walk
        toward
        the house.

FAITH

I love
riding
my bike,
especially
at night.

On
darkened
streets
like a
low-flying
bird
soaring
along
just above
the pavement.

Almost
invisible.

I snuck
out of
the house.
It was
Emma
who taught
me how:
to avoid the

third stair
from the top,
to ease the
screen door
shut.

When
I came
downstairs
I could
hear the TV
on in the
family room.

Polly almost
ruined
everything
with a
plaintive,
drawn-out,
don't-go
whimper
when she
followed me
down to
the kitchen.

Quietly
I roll
my bike
out the

side door
of the
garage.

On the
sidewalk
in front
of our
house,
my bicycle
wheel
bumps over
something,
something
that makes
a faint
squeaking
sound.

I lean over.
It's a
black rubber
crow,
with a grimy
yellow beak.
Polly's
favorite
chew toy,
faded,
gnawed on,
well loved.

Don't know
how it got
out here
on the front
sidewalk.
I stick it
in the
back pocket
of my shorts,
and it
squeaks,
softly.

I know
the streets
of this town
by heart,
from riding
my bike.

Holding the
handlebars
one-handed,
I flip open
my cell.
After
midnight.
But there's
still time
to stop
Emma.

To warn
her.

It's a
sultry night.
Leftover heat
from the day
rises up
from the
sidewalk,
but the
rushing air
on my face
feels good.

There's a
movie
about a boy
in a small
Midwest town
who loves
to bike.
It's my
all-time
favorite
movie.
He pretends
he's Italian,
the way
I pretend

I'm just like
everyone else.

Here is
what I say
every day
when I get
on my bike:

Ciao, bellissimo Midwestern town of Wilmette.

I pretend
I'm off
to Italy,
or London,
or Seattle,
or California.

In just
four years,
I really will
be gone,
so fast
everyone
will choke
on the dust
from my
bicycle wheels
as I ride
out of town.

Off to new
wide-open
worlds
where a girl
can be
who she is
meant
to be.

But for now,
in this place
and this time,
I'm here.

And I can't
let it all
crumble
beneath me.

WALTER

They're out there. The bad guys. I can hear them.
    Their voices, the sound of the car idling.
Through the trees I can see flickering lights
    coming up the path toward our house.

A sheriff has to protect his town,
    but he has to protect his home as well.
There is no one but me to do it.
    I move toward the closet.

FELIX

we watch emma and chloe go slowly, very slowly, up the
crumbling stone steps to the path leading to the house.
max is freaked out. i want to tell her not to care so much.
to just let things go.

Remember Joey Pigza? I ask softly.

max looks at me, her eyes wild, scared.

Who?
Those books I read over and over, I say. *In 5th grade.*
Oh yeah, she says after a moment.

brendan is still texting, intent on the keyboard cradled in
his hand. i hear chloe's giggles drifting back as max and i
watch the light from the two cell phones bobbing slowly
toward the house.

Joey Pigza was always doing stupid shit like this, I say.
    And he survived.
Joey Pigza, Max murmurs. *He was the one with ADHD?*
Yeah, like me. Hey, Max, I say, with a big grin, *did I*
    ever tell you how someday I'm going to do research
    and prove that weed is the best medicine for ADHD?

max smiles.

Good luck with that, she says.

Actually, comes Anil's voice from the back, *it's not a bad idea.*
Really? I say

i turn around to look at him, surprised.

Yeah, some doctors in California prescribe medical marijuana for ADHD, but there's very little research to . . .

another set of chloe giggles. louder.

Be quiet, Chloe, comes Emma's voice, clear and annoyed. Loud. Too loud.

anil stops talking and max's smile disappears. her hands are clenched tight on the armrests and i'm suddenly tired of this whole thing. what the hell are we doing here? i should get max home, out of this.

Hey, Brendan, I say, leaning forward, *this is lame. Can you get your girlfriend back here so we can all go home.*

brendan turns and glares at me. looking at his slack mouth and dilated, glittering eyes, i suddenly realize how out-of-his-mind blitzed he is.

Go back to your weed, dickhead. Emma wants her fun.
Oh, that's right. I forgot, I say. *You do whatever Emma wants, don't you?*

i lock eyes with him. max darts a scared glance at me. like

what the hell are you doing? her face says. and she's right.
brendan looks like he's ready to tear my eyeballs out. but
i can't help it. this i-own-the-planet, gun-toting asshole
is seriously messing with EMFAX. god, did i just call us
EMFAX again? that's the third time tonight. i must be
more messed up than i thought.

> *Shut the fuck up, you pathetic slacker loser,* Brendan
> says, *or else . . .*

and like in a dream i see his hand reaching toward the
glove compartment. behind us, anil lets out a sharp exhale.
and *NO!* bursts from max's throat. brendan looks back at
the three of us. he knows we know and his eyes go to slits.

he pops open the glove compartment and in the blink of
an eye that shiny black gun is in brendan's hand.

BRENDAN

I can't believe those pussies went rooting
around in my glove compartment.

And who does that useless pothead
think he is, mouthing off to me like that.

Like he's my fucking asshole dad.
I should fucking scare the crap out of them.

Serves them right.

MAXIE

I feel like I'm in a bad movie,
one with a jittery
handheld
camera
recording everything.
     Including a monster
     lurking in the shadows.

Except
maybe the
monster
is sitting right there
in front of us.

Brendan is grinning,
waving his
gun.

      You know what kind of gun this is? he says. *A*
         double-action semiautomatic Beretta 92 F.
      Put it away, Brendan, says Felix softly.
      Hell no. Teach you a lesson, Brendan says, his words
         slurring.

Suddenly Brendan reaches up
and punches a button
next to the moonroof.
The glass panel

silently
slides
open . . . .

Then he thrusts up his hand,
the one holding the gun,
through the opening
to the night sky.

EMMA

Dare you to touch the door, says Chloe, giggling again.

She's stopped halfway up the path
to the front door,
blocking my way.

And then suddenly
from the direction of the car
comes a loud popping sound.

> *What was that?* Chloe cries out, turning and
> stumbling toward me.

I try to catch her, but she trips on
a pot of flowers, knocking it over
with a noisy clattering sound.

She flounders, trying to recover her balance,
(Chloe always was the world's biggest klutz),
and somehow she kicks over another one.

> *OW!* she says, way too loud, falling sideways onto
> the grass.

I hear the shattering sound
of a third pot breaking,
Chloe's breath coming quickly.

I hurt my foot, Chloe bleats.
Go back to the car, I say, helping her up.
I think it's bleeding, she says.
Go back, I whisper. *I'll be there in a sec.*

Chloe limps her way back down the path.
Even though I know it's reckless, I have to go on.
I have to know if there's a ghost.

My cell light fades,
so I tap the keypad.
Light blooms.

I can see the broken pots,
pink roses and dirt tumbled out
onto the path.

A lot of the flowers are flattened from
Chloe trampling on them. Then I hear a
soft sighing sound. From the house.

> *Who's there?* comes a whispery, plaintive voice.

I see a screen door, with jagged tears in the
metal netting. And behind the screen door
a woman is standing. White hair haloing a shadowed face.

> *My roses. Don't hurt my roses.*

The voice is thin, worried. Unearthly.

She moves toward me, her gnarled hands
reaching through the screen like it's not there.

For just a moment I believe she *is* a ghost.
But then I see she is reaching through the rips in the screen.
A real-life old woman in a shapeless nightgown.

I am suddenly ashamed.
This is a person, a living breathing person
whose flowers we've ruined.

I'm sorry, I whisper and back away.

She opens the screen door,
goes through, letting it fall shut behind her
with a sharp thunking sound.

I keep moving backward. She follows me
down the path. But she stops abruptly
in front of the first broken pot.

She crouches beside it.
And then I see her face crumple,
her mouth gaping open.

I hear a high-pitched wailing,
so agonized and unearthly that at first
I don't realize it's coming from her.

MOTHER! shouts another voice, urgent, coming
from inside the house.

My heart starts pounding.

Oh god.

What have I done?

MAXIE

When Brendan sticks
his gun
up through the moonroof
and deliberately lets off
two shots,
my whole body goes
numb.

The shots are loud,
painfully
deafeningly
       loud.

I can see Felix's lips move,
but can barely hear
the words.

He reaches over
and takes hold of my
       ice-cold hand.

       Put the gun away, Brendan, I hear Anil say through
       the buzzing in my ears.

His voice is strong,
level.

Brendan swivels his head around

to look back
at Anil.

What's wrong, Paki? Did I scare you? he asks, voice
mocking.

Suddenly the door next to Felix
opens
and Chloe's there.
Her face is crumpled,
wet with
tears.

I cut my foot, she says.

I look down
and see
blood
pooling up between
her toes,
covering the straps of
her silvery sandals.

Then comes
the scream,
and we all
freeze.

What the . . . Brendan breathes, clutching his
    gun tighter.
Jesus, Felix says, dropping my hand. *Emma . . .*

Felix is out the door,
so fast
it's like he
       disappeared.

Then Emma
is running
toward us.
She is pointing Felix
back toward
the car.

We need to get out of here, she says. *Now.*

Chloe tumbles past me
to the backseat,
next to Anil.
Felix slams his door shut,
sliding into the seat next to me.
His eyes are fixed on
Emma.

Go, Brendan, Emma says, voice urgent.

Then she spots the
gun
in his hand.

What the hell? she says, eyes wide.

But Brendan doesn't let go of

the gun.
He turns on the engine,
puts the car into drive,
and
accelerates.

Then he deliberately
sticks his hand
up through the open moonroof—
a parting shot.

So loud my hearing goes
dim again.

Emma, her face livid with rage,
knocks
the gun
out of his hand.
It clatters to the floor,
at my feet.
Without even thinking
I kick it under my seat.

A few seconds later,
    a horrible,
    terrifying,
    catastrophic
    answer:
loud popping noises
coming from the house.
Then more.

Louder!
Like the sound of
fireworks.

Behind me,
or beside Felix,
it's hard to tell,
comes the sound of
    glass
      shattering.

And, right after that,
in front of me,
the windshield suddenly is
      blurred, cracked.

Felix lets out
a soft grunt,
almost like
a sigh.

Brendan is weaving,
swearing.

Then Emma screams.

    Stop the car! It's <u>Faith</u>.

Faith?
How could Faith be
    here??

FAITH

I smell:

    new mown grass
    the sweet perfume of flowers,
    roses, I think.

I see:

    cemetery gates
    and down the block
    Brendan's SUV,
    idling.

I hear:

    the steady drone of cicadas
    then a few muffled popping noises
    something breaking
    a car door slamming
    a scream
    more popping, louder and closer,
    much closer.

I feel:

    the handlebars of my bike tilt
    the sidewalk rushing up at me
    pain, unexpected
        overwhelming

I taste:

    blood in my mouth

MAXIE

Emma yells again at Brendan.

STOP THE CAR!

But it's like he
hasn't heard.

Emma opens her door
anyway,
jumps out,
while it's still
moving,
fast!

I watch her fall,
hard,
onto the sidewalk.

Then she's up,
tries to stand,
but her right leg
collapses
beneath her,
and she is on the ground.

Once again
she rises,
teetering on her left leg,

hopping back toward
the ghost house.

Brendan, stop! I shout.

He jams on the brake.
Tires squeal
and we're all jerked
forward.

I look back.
Emma has stopped
and is leaning over
something lying
on the ground.

Brendan wrenches open his car door
and stumbles out into
the street.

Felix, I start, turning toward him.

But Felix is slumped forward,
the seat belt the only thing
holding him up.
With an icy jolt of horror
I see
blood
dripping
into
his lap.

ANIL

1. Chloe, beside me,
crying.
Wiping the blood
from her foot with Kleenex.
A lot of blood
so I'm thinking it
must be a bad cut,
maybe needs stitches,
and I lean toward her
to see if I can help.

2. Then the window beside Felix
splinters,
and the front windshield
is suddenly a spiderweb of cracks.

I look at Maxie, her face in profile,
and it is dead white,
her eyes wide with shock.

Felix, she whispers, reaching toward him.

I see the blood then
on Felix's headrest,
and, without thinking,
I'm beside him.

3. Gaping wound,

on the side of his head,
where his right eye
was.

Feel for a pulse.
It's there.
Thin and thready,
but there.

Call 911, I say to Maxie. *Now.*

I tear off my shirt.
Wad it up. Gently press it
against the wound.
Felix groans.
Looking into his other eye,
I see immense pain.

Sorry, Felix. Hang in there, I say, trying to keep
my voice calm, reassuring.

4. Maxie's hands are shaking,
    but she's got 911 on the line.

Someone's hurt. Shot, I think, she says, her voice
surprisingly steady.

Can hear the crackle
of an answering voice.

Near Walnut Creek Cemetery, Maxie says.

McKinley Road . . . In the head . . . Might be more
than one person . . .

She's looking out the window
at Emma, who is crouched
beside a still figure
sprawled on the sidewalk.

Hurry please, Maxie says.

Chloe hovers beside me.

Can I help?
Hold this, I say.

And without hesitating,
Chloe puts her hand where I guide it,
to the wadded-up shirt
quickly filling up
with blood.

5. Gently I begin lowering the back
of Felix's seat.

I've got to go to Emma, Maxie says. *They want*
   to know . . .
No, Maxie, I say, urgent, *a shooter's out there.*
I know, she says. *But it's Faith.*

She squeezes by, out of the car,
and disappears.

MAXIE

I spot the bike first,
the front tire
blown out,
spokes bent
    and twisted.

Faith is lying half under it,
Emma bent
over her.

    Faith! Faith, can you hear me? Emma is saying.

Faith's eyes are closed.
There's
blood
on her face,
and more,
a lot more,
on the leg that's pinned
at an awkward angle,
    under the bike.

Brendan is beside Emma,
his body taut,
alert.

    She was awake, talking to me, Emma is saying to
      Brendan, *and then she just sort of stopped, and her*

eyes closed . . .
We need to get the bike off her, Brendan says.

There is no trace of
slurring
in his words.

And in one easy movement
he lifts the bicycle off
Faith,
as if it's no heavier than
a feather.

Then he turns back to
Emma.

Emma, he says, *get back to the car. You, too,* he adds,
looking in my direction.

The drunken, slack-mouthed
evil Brendan
is gone.

In a matter of moments,
he has changed into
the lacrosse team captain.
　　　Strong.
　　　In charge.

I turn to go back to the SUV.
But Emma isn't moving,

focused only on
her sister.

I think I feel a pulse, she says. *But there's so much*
   blood . . .
I'll stay with her. Go back to the car, Brendan repeats.

Emma shakes her head,
refusing to leave.

I notice she is holding something
tightly in her hand.
Something dark,
covered with
blood.
It looks like
   a toy.

Brendan crouches down,
beside Emma,
looking her straight in the eye.
Despite the faint ringing
still in my ears,
I can hear
   every word.

There's someone with a gun, at the ghost house, he says
   deliberately. *You and Maxie need to get back to*
   the car.
No, is all Emma says.
An ambulance is on the way, Brendan says.

And it's then that I notice
the sound of
sirens
in the distance.

Emma stays where she is.

Faith, you're gonna be all right. I'm here, she says.

Brendan looks at me,
his face
dead serious,
and makes a gesture
with his hand
        toward the SUV.

I go,
but looking behind me,
I see Brendan,
with that same easy strength
        lifting Emma
        into his arms.

She flails against him,
though it's clear that her own
        right leg is
        badly hurt.

Suddenly she jerks so hard
he can't hold her,
and she's

on the ground,
then up again,
hopping on her good leg
back to Faith.

EMMA

I am squeezing the rubber crow,
Polly's favorite chew toy,
tight in my hand.

It's smeared with blood, Faith's blood.
Oh please God,
let Faith be okay.

BRENDAN

I start to follow Emma,
then hear Anil calling out to me.

Brendan, watch out, is what I hear.

I spin toward the ghost house and see
the figure of a man moving toward us.

Or maybe it's a boy.
With a rifle in his hands.

Emma, I call instinctively, to warn her.

She turns, then freezes,
staring at the figure holding the rifle.

She raises her hand,
the one holding the bloody crow,

As if to fend off
what's about to happen.

I see the rifle go up,
pointing straight at Emma.

And I move.

MAXIE

I watch as
Brendan collides with Emma,
    knocking her off her feet.

And at the very same second
that their bodies meet,
    one last shot rings out,
    splitting the night
      wide open.

AFTER

POLICE CHIEF AUBREY DELAFIELD

Even before I answer
the phone, I know.

I don't know how I know,
but I do.
Something has happened,
something big, something life-changing.
And not in a good way.

I arrive on McKinley Road two seconds behind
the first ambulance.
I say first because it was clear
from the initial 911 call
that we were gonna need more than one.
A lot more.

MAXIE

I keep telling them
I'm not hurt,
that it's not
blood
on my shirt,
    it's
      MoonBuzz.

Then I realize.
It <u>is</u>
blood.
    Felix's
    blood.

A man with pale eyelashes
is talking to me,
his voice calm.

    I'm not hurt, I keep saying.

Finally he looks me
in the eye
and says softly,

    You're in shock.

Which shuts me up.
Because,

yes,
that's exactly what
I am.
In shock.

And likely to remain that way
for a
long,
long
time.

CHLOE

"Blood and Sandals"

Sitting on the curb,
I have this weird
peaceful drowsy feeling,
even though my foot throbs like
my beating heart has slid down into it,
and blood is pooling
under my sandal.
A lot of blood.
(That sandal is going
to be ruined and
it's too bad because
those silver sandals
are my favorites.)

There are flashing lights
and cars and people
rushing around.

Someone shines a light in my eyes.
Someone else is talking to me,
asking what my name is
and what the date is,
like I really care about that
right now.

The boy next to me has started to cry

and I feel sorry for him,
but I wish everyone would just
shut up and go away
because all I really want to do
is
go
to
sleep.

WALTER

If Billy Clanton had only surrendered
   a lot of bloodshed would have been spared.
But the town must be protected and
   a sheriff has to make the tough choices.

The girl with the yellow hair, sitting by me on the curb,
   she understood.
Mother. Where is Mother?
   Billy Clanton had a gun. I saw the gun in his hand.

But the thing I picked up. It was a toy, not a gun.
   A rubber toy. That squeaks.
The toy is wet, with Billy's blood? Or someone else's?
   It was a girl. My head hurts. I don't know.

Mother. I need to keep Mother safe
   from the bad guys, from the Clantons.
Need to stay strong, protect Mother.
   What do all these people want?

But I recognized the girl. The girl covered in blood.
   The girl on the bike. I've seen her, with her dog.
She was a good guy, at least I thought so.
   Someone you could be friends with.

MOTHER?

POLICE CHIEF AUBREY DELAFIELD

A pale slight kid wearing
a baggy green sweatshirt and glasses
is sitting on the curb,
holding a blood-smeared
rubber crow
in his hands,
crying.

And a pale blonde girl with a bloody foot
sits beside him, her hand
resting on his shoulder.

Even though he's small and thin,
he looks to be about the same age
as the blonde girl and the other kids.
But I can tell right away he is separate,
not with them.

And it's not because he's so skinny
or pale
or wearing glasses
that are too large for his face.

The other kids are in shock,
disoriented.
But this kid, he's got a look on his face
like he has no idea
how he got here,

what just happened.
Lost.

I approach him carefully.

All I can see is
this rubber crow in his hands.
But I'm sure there's a weapon,
somewhere nearby.

He looks up at me
with his wet eyes,
then points,
like he can read my mind.

And, sure enough, there it is,
lying on the sidewalk.
A rifle.

ANIL

1. I want to ride
    In the ambulance
    with Felix.
    But they won't let me.

    The police chief says
    he needs me to stay,
    to help him sort out
    what happened here.

    As if I know.

MAXIE

The man with the
pale eyelashes
says I need to follow him to
   an ambulance.

   I'm not hurt, I say again, like those are the only words
   I know anymore.

But what I really mean is:

   I can't move.

Since my feet
are suddenly
not my feet,
but unmovable
blocks of concrete
attached to the bottom of
my legs.

My head,
on the other hand,
feels light,
buzzy.
like it might
   float away.

Then I see

Emma
on a stretcher,
her face the color of
streaky white marble,
her eyes closed and
her arm connected
    by a tube
    to a bag
    on a pole.

And after that,
    everything
      goes
          dark.

ANIL

1. Chief Delafield steps away
to talk to another cop,
and an EMT guy
wearing a black shirt
with a logo I can't make out
comes over with a couple of towels for me.

And I suddenly remember
I'm not wearing a shirt,
that I'd used my shirt on Felix,
and that my chest and arms
are streaked with his blood.

In a daze I wipe myself with the towel,
but I suddenly feel weak,
exhausted, and stop,
draping the towel around
my neck to hide my nakedness.

2. I stare out at the scene before me,
then look at my watch.
But I can't read it through
the splotches of blood, still wet,
on the watch face.

Time has blurred,
Maxie could've called 911

a few minutes ago,
or a few hours.
I don't know anymore.

But in the space of that time,
or at least since
the first ambulance arrived,
a small city of vans and cars
and flashing lights
and yellow tape
has mushroomed
around us.

Staccato bursts of
walkie-talkie voices,
urgent, saying things like
perimeter secured,
shooter in custody.

And real voices, also urgent
and hoarse, saying things like
airway clear,
pressure dropping,
c-spine secure.

3.   Then, out of the corner
of my eye,
I see Maxie fall,
limp and pale,
to the ground.

Instinctively I move toward her,
but an EMT guy stops me.

We've got her, son.

4.   Chief Delafield is back.
He leads me toward the SUV.

First thing I need from you, Anil, he says, *are the
names and addresses of all the kids who were with
you in the car.*

I know why.
So their parents can be
notified.

Your kid was shot tonight.
And might die.

I shiver,
then start talking.

MAXIE

I wake up in the
    ambulance.

You fainted, says the man in his calm voice.

And the image of
Emma's
marble face
comes back with a rush.
I concentrate on
    breathing.

Then I see the IV
attached to the
back of
my hand.

I feel this flash of
    outrage.

    I don't need that, I say.
    Just a precaution, the man says.
    Take it off, I say.

Inside I'm screaming,

    You don't understand. I'm not the one who got shot!

We arrive at the hospital
and I'm taken
in a wheelchair
to the ER.

I've always been
scared of hospitals.
They make me think of
        death.

But everyone is so nice,
so reassuring.

They wheel me into
an empty room,
and take some
blood
for a tox screen,
whatever that is.

        Just a precaution, they say.

I keep asking about Felix
and Emma
and Faith.
Over and over:
        where are they?
        how are they?

But no one will tell me
anything.

FAITH

Being pulled
onward,
like Polly
pulling me
forward
on her leash.

But I
can't see
Polly,
only
a soft
whiteness
all around
me.

Quiet,
like
swimming
underwater,
but even
more
silent.

Movement
against
my face,
around

my body.
Soft, gentle
white birds,
like ivory gulls,
all around,
surrounding
me.

Nothing sharp,
no beaks
or claws,
just feathers,
lightly
brushing
my
face,
and
arms
and legs.

Calm and
loving
and
sweet.

POLICE CHIEF AUBREY DELAFIELD

There was a case
back five years ago,
a young man who strangled his mother,
and then shot himself.

That was a tough
crime scene to process.
But it doesn't hold a candle
to this one.
Not even close.

Five kids hurt,
four in ICU,
three with injuries so bad
they could quite possibly
die before morning.

The Indian kid, Anil Sayanantham,
walks me through what happened
as best he can.

It's clear he's in shock and
I hate to put him through this,
but I've got to get at
the truth, as quickly as possible.
Even if none of those kids die,
God willing,

the media is going to be
all over this.

A real circus,
I can feel it coming.

But I can't think about that right now.
Need to concentrate on
getting this job done
and getting it done right.

Sergeant Wilcox drives off
with the perp,
this boy who picked up a gun
and shot up a car full of teenagers,
and one on a bike.
This pale skinny boy
who can't stop crying.

Who will take care of Mother?

That's the last thing he says,
sobbing, before they drive away.

So I go up the path,
past three broken pots of roses.
Enter the house, through a screen door
with holes in the mesh.

The house is dead quiet. Dark.
I find myself reaching for my firearm.

Then I see a faint light coming
from the second floor.
So I head toward the staircase.

But just before I step on that first stair,
I hear a sound. The sound of a chair,
rocking.

From the dim light coming from above,
I see the living room, to my right.
And a figure of
a white-haired lady
sitting in an upholstered rocking chair.
Rocking.

She has her hands cupped
in front of her, and is staring down,
unblinking, absorbed by what she sees
in her hands.

Ma'am? I say.

She looks up, then lifts her hands toward me,
as if offering me something.

My roses, she says. *They broke my roses.*

I can just barely make out a pile of
bruised pink rose petals
cupped carefully
in her hands.

MAXIE

When Mom and Dad
come into the hospital room
I suddenly
start to cry and
    can't stop.

Like one of those weird
face fountains
you see in pictures of gardens in Italy,
with the water
endlessly trickling from
    unseeing
    stone eyes.

The tears come
and come
and come,
until my body is doubled over
with sobs
so hard my
    ribs hurt.

Mom takes me
in her arms
like I'm six years old again.

    It's going to be okay, she murmurs.

Dad hovers behind her.

Maxie, Maxie, Maxie, he's saying, his voice hoarse
with his love.

They're trying to hide it
but both of them look
    terrified.

I want to stop
the wrenching sobs,
    but I can't.

Then the door opens
and a man in a sport coat
enters the room.
He gestures to my dad,
who steps toward him.
    They talk,
    voices low.

Then they both turn to face me.
My stomach clenches.
    Has someone died?
    Is the shooter still out there?

Dad crosses to me,
puts his hand
on my back.

Maxie, he says. *They want to know about Felix's*

parents. No one answered when they went to his house.
Do you know if they're out of town?

I hesitate for a moment,
but they need to know
    the truth.

Through hiccupping tears
I explain about
    Felix's dad in Afghanistan,
    and how his mother is depressed
    and takes sleeping pills.

Dad looks sad.

    Poor Felix, he murmurs.

I nod,
fresh tears
filling
my eyes.

    Is he . . . ? I say, looking at the cop.
    In surgery, he says, his face drawn. *Thanks for your*
        help. He starts to leave, then turns to face me again.
        Also, when you're feeling up to it, we're going to need
        you to come down to the police station. Tonight. Just a
        few questions.

I nod again,
not even aware

anymore
of the tears
streaming down
    my face.

ANIL

1.   After the police station
    I wanted to stop at the hospital,
    but my mom said no.

     You need sleep, she says.

    But sleep doesn't come.
    And as I lie in my bed,
    wide awake, I wonder
    if it ever will again.

2.   I look up at
    the glow-in-the-dark stars
    my mom put on my
    bedroom ceiling when
    I was in elementary school.

    Back in 4th grade I learned
    about the big bang theory
    and the beginnings
    of the universe,
    and I came up with this game
    I'd play in my head,
    a game of finding
    the beginnings of things.

    Some beginnings are simple.
    Some are more complex.

But when I was in 4th grade
I was pretty good at
tracing things back
to a single moment.

And, right now, I need to find
the beginning of this thing that happened
to me, to all of us, tonight.

Was it when Chloe knocked over the flowerpots?
Or when I popped open the glove compartment?
Or when Felix spilled the MoonBuzz on Maxie's
lavender shirt?
Or when Chloe said, let's go ghosting?
Or when Brendan bought MoonBuzz on
Craigslist?

Or was it when the first kid looked at that run-
down house across from a cemetery and decided
it was scary, called it 'the ghost house,' and dared
some other kid to go near it? A run-down house
where a boy and his grandmother live, a boy who
wears glasses and who owns a gun.

It suddenly is imperative
that I find the beginning.

Because that would
be the moment
I could have stopped all this
from happening.

MAXIE

When I entered
the police station
Anil was leaving with
      his parents.

They had brought
him a fresh shirt,
to replace the bloody one.
I could see
ironed creases
crisscrossing
the front of the
white shirt.
I could also see
brown-red streaks
on his forearms.

Our eyes met.
His were deep black pools of
fatigue and shock.
Mine felt sandpapery red,
swollen, and I had to
look away.

I was at the police station
until four in the morning.

It seemed impossible

at first
to put what had taken place
that night into a
    this-happened,
    that-happened
    narrative.

But Police Chief Delafield
led me through it,
with a no-nonsense
gentleness
that at least kept
the tears from
    starting
    up
    again.

It was weird how
I'd remember a tiny detail,
like the smell of
sage
in the cemetery,
but forget big things,
like:
what happened to
Brendan's gun
    (under the seat),
how far from the house
we were when the
windshield cracked and split
    (not far),

did Emma hold up the
rubber crow
before or after
Walter Smith pointed his rifle
at her
        (before).

They took
        (confiscated)
my camera.

I watched them put it
in a plastic bag,
put a label on it,
seal it,
drop it in a bin,
and for a moment
I had trouble
        breathing.

That camera is almost
always
with me,
or has been for the
past four years.
A best friend,
a part of my body.
And now it is
flecked with blood
and sealed in plastic
with a label

that reads
EVIDENCE.

After we got home,
I took
a shower,
burning hot,
went to bed and
let sleep,
faceless and blank,
pull me under.

POLICE CHIEF AUBREY DELAFIELD

I put in a call to Jeremy Sisto,
Principal of George Washington High School.

I've known Jeremy twenty years.
And he knew right away
it wasn't a social call,
not this early on a Sunday morning.

He's a good man, Jeremy Sisto,
and a good principal.
He'll handle what needs to be done
with efficiency and intelligence.

Crisis-management teams
will be poised and ready
to swing into action on
Monday morning,
when kids arrive at
George Washington High School
for their first day of school.

Their first day in a world
that will surely feel a whole lot
less safe,
less predictable
than it did
the day before.

ANIL

1. Finally I get out of bed.
And even though I've
already washed
and scrubbed my arms
and hands until they're raw,
I go into the bathroom
and do it all over again.

Then,
grabbing car keys,
I slip out the back door
of our house.

2. The sun is about to rise,
an eyelash of bright light
on the horizon.

The hospital entry is quiet.
I can smell breakfast
being cooked somewhere.

A tired-looking receptionist
with pinched lips informs me
that she can't give out any
information.

I stare at her, frustrated.
Maybe if I told her I was there,

in that SUV, holding Felix's head in my arms.
Maybe then she'd tell me if he was still alive.

But she ignores me standing there,
unsmiling, cold.
As if fatigue and fear
have erased her ability
to be kind, at least in this moment.

3. I stand paralyzed.
    Then a nurse, sturdy,
    with blonde hair cut short,
    comes up to me.
    She takes my arm, leading me
    away from the pinched receptionist.

    Her name tag says GEORGIA,
    and in a quiet voice she tells me
    that Felix is still in surgery.
    Same for Faith and Emma.

    She doesn't know anything
    about Brendan,
    thinks maybe he was airlifted
    to another hospital.

    She points me to
    a waiting room,
    then surprises me
    with a hug.

For a moment
I am afraid I will collapse,
fall to my knees and sob,
out of control
right here in front of
this nurse named Georgia.

But I manage to keep myself still,
face blank,
and thank her.

4. I find the room and enter.
   The only people there are
   a man and woman,
   looking exhausted,
   frightened, holding hands.

   I know right away they are
   Emma and Faith's parents.

   The dad looks up,
   about to say something,
   when the door behind me opens.

   A doctor in surgical scrubs,
   his face gray with fatigue,
   moves past me, toward the couple.

   They stand, stricken, wobbly,
   like they can barely stay upright.

Just finished surgery. Emma's in ICU, I can hear
the doctor say.

Even though I want to hear more,
I feel like I'm intruding,
so I move toward the door.

*She's critical but stable . . . concussion . . . leg
fractured in several places . . . will need more
surgery* are the words I can make out.

Then the woman asks,
her voice cracking,

And Faith?
Still in surgery. Sorry.

POLICE CHIEF AUBREY DELAFIELD

The inside of that SUV
was a secondary crime scene
so we towed it to the station.

The pools of blood
and car windows with bullet holes
told the broad outline,
but the gun under the seat,
with four spent rounds,
the cooler of illegal booze
disguised as a harmless sports drink,
the burnt end of
a couple of reefers
filled in the rest of the story.

The statements we took
from Anil Sayanantham
and Maxine Kalman, and later,
Chloe Carney
all dovetailed.

Even the words that came out of
the boy's mouth, the boy named
Walter Smith,
told the same story.
But from a very different
point of view.

Trespassers. True.

Potential home invaders. Not true.

A gun fired toward the house. True.

Had to protect myself and my mother. Not true.

No. That was not true at all.

EMMA

The sun is a blazing ball
of pulsing white
in a vivid blue sky.

The soccer field
is emerald green,
brighter than I've ever seen it.

I'm dribbling a ball down the field.
Defenders are little buzzing dots
Far, far behind me.

The goal is wide open, waiting.
I feel that exhilarating,
familiar rush of certainty.

I swing my leg back
and, *thunk*, the gleaming
black-and-white ball soars.

It traces a perfect arc over
the goalie, landing smack
in the center of the goal.

A roar from the bleachers.
I look up, see Mom and Dad
on their feet, cheering.

Then I look for Faith.
She's not there.
Fear stabs me in the gut.

And that's when I wake up.
Faith!
I feel a hand take mine.

Honey, Emma, a voice says. *It's Mom.*

I open my eyes.

MAXIE

When I wake up
the house is
        quiet.

I lie in bed,
groggy from such a long sleep.
        Not knowing if it's morning or afternoon.
        Not remembering.

And then I do.

I stumble out of bed
to the bathroom.
Leaning over the toilet,
I heave
and heave
until nothing more
        comes out.

Mom hears me
and runs in,
wrapping her arms
around me.
Wiping my hot face
with a cool washcloth.

Later

we're sitting at
the breakfast table,
Mom and Dad and I,
and they tell me what
they know
          so far.

That Emma is in
critical condition,
but expected to
          survive.

That the last they heard,
Faith was still in surgery.
And it didn't
          look good.

That nobody seems to know
about Brendan.
They think
he's at another hospital,
          in Chicago.

          And Felix? I ask, my heart pounding.

And that's when
they tell me.

That Felix survived.
He came through
surgery,

but he lost
    his right eye
    (like an eye was something
    you could carelessly lose).
And now,
he
is in
a
coma.

Brain trauma
is a tricky thing,
    they say.

He may never wake up,
    they say.

And if he does wake up,
he may never be
    the same.

Or he could be
fine.
At least as
fine
as you can be
with only
one
eye.

POLICE CHIEF AUBREY DELAFIELD

His name is Walter Smith.
Nineteen years of age.
Five foot seven inches,
barely 130 pounds,
brown hair.

He was born at 6 a.m.
on a Sunday morning,
January 16.
No father listed
on the birth certificate.
Mabel Smith
is listed as the mother.

No known address
for a Mabel Smith,
though she has a record:
several arrests
for drug possession,
public intoxication,
and disturbing the peace,
but that was all
twenty years ago.

Walter Smith was
raised by his grandmother,
Adeline Smith,

the woman he calls
Mother.

She's homeschooled him since
the age of eleven,
in the house she inherited
from her sister.

The two,
Walter and Adeline Smith,
have always kept to themselves.
But according to neighbors
there have been escalating
signs of dementia
in the grandmother:

> -sitting on the front stoop, arguing loudly with her
> dead sister
> -wearing a winter down parka as she gardens in the
> hot summer sun
> -dancing in her nightgown in the tangled
> undergrowth of the neglected property.

Numerous complaints
by neighbors
about the deteriorating house and yard.
Numerous complaints
by the grandmother
about being harassed
by neighborhood kids.
And even though I didn't know

it was called the "ghost house"
and that neighborhood kids
used it to scare themselves,
I can't say I wasn't aware
of the house, of these people.
I was.
But I confess I thought
they were harmless.
Eccentric.
And that the people around them
should just
live and let live.

God's truth,
I was blind.
Well, that's something
I'm going to have to
live with until the day
I die.

MAXIE

Word spreads fast
about what happened
at the
    ghost house.

And Sunday night,
the night after it happened,
there is a vigil
at the school.
    For Brendan,
      for Emma and Faith,
      and for Felix.

Hundreds of kids
fill the
    football field.

I hadn't wanted
to go—
    not at first.

But Mom and Dad
said they'd go with me.
Wanted to go with me.
    And so I said
    okay.

There are news trucks
and camera crews,
which Mom and
Dad hurry me past.

I sit in the bleachers
with Mom on one side
and Dad on the other
and hope no one will
        recognize me.

And because I am
the new/old girl,
        they don't.

The whole thing is overwhelming,
but somehow beautiful, too,
all these people
gathered together,
shaken to the core,
        mourning,
            and frightened.

And then they start
lighting
        candles.

First one,
then a few,
then more and more.
Till the field is

filled with
    flickering candles.

I don't have
my camera (still confiscated),
but Dad has loaned me his,
and Mom smiles
when I click a photo
of that
    winking,
    sparkling
    sea of light.

Dad takes my hand
and that's when
I burst into tears.
    Again.

I spot Chloe's
blonde hair
across the field.
She's surrounded by friends.
But no sign of
Anil.

And for some reason,
out of the blue,
I suddenly remember
Anil's story about the comet
and the
two telescopes,

and
his smile,
and then,
miraculously,
　　my tears stop.

ANIL

1. My parents don't want me
    to go to the vigil,
    which is okay
    because I don't want to go.

    The only reason would've
    been to see if Maxie was there.
    Except what would
    I say to her?

2. I watch TV and go on the Internet,
    scrolling from one story to
    another about the tragic
    shooting in Wilmette.

    Sound bites have already formed:
        multiple shooting victims near cemetery
        tragedy at so-called "ghost house"
        homeschooled boy shoots rifle at trespassing
          teens
        teenage prank gone wrong
        thrill-seeking, ghost-hunting teens

    But no word on:
        Felix
        Faith
        Emma
        or Brendan.

Nothing specific anyway.
Just "multiple victims" in critical condition.
That's all.

Mom turns off the TV
but I turn it back on.
She looks at me,
then sits beside me,
putting her arm
around my shoulders.

One news program shows
clusters of reporters
from different TV stations
around the country,
camped in front of the hospital.

3. And then,
while we're watching TV,
a knock on our own door.
Reporters.
My father turns them away,
tight-lipped, furious.

EMMA

Dad is sitting by my bed.
The machines around me are whirring,
tubes, wires, dials sprouting from them.

The tubes are filled with bubbling liquids that are
being pumped into me, to help me heal,
to help control the pain.

Dad is telling me about the vigil at the
football field tonight. How everyone is
praying for me, for Faith, for all of us.

The hospital room is filled with cards and
flowers and balloons. Almost too bright,
too much, and I don't deserve any of it.

Faith? I keep asking. And they keep
telling me they don't know. That she's
still fighting, still alive.

Then the door opens, abruptly,
making Dad jump.
A nurse stands there.

> *You're to come, right now,* she says.

Her voice is urgent,
her eyes unreadable,

but she is not smiling.

Dad jumps up.
I can see fear
in his eyes.

I'll be right back, Emma, he says.

Just as the door closes behind them I hear
the words *minister or priest?* clear and distinct.
My blood turns to ice.

Faith, I shout.

MAXIE

On Monday instead of going
to school
I go to
    the hospital.

Mom and I get flowers
from the grocery store
to take to
    Emma,
    Faith,
    and Felix

Faith's room is the closest
so we go there
first.

The door is
closed.

I hear the sound of a woman
sobbing
and my brain goes blank.

I drop the flowers and
don't even realize it.

Suddenly the door

opens
and Emma's dad is
standing there.

He stares at me
and all the flowers
    scattered at my feet.

Then
he smiles.
I look past him into the room
and see Faith and Emma's mom
sitting by the bed,
and she's not sobbing,
she's laughing,
though
    tears are running
    down her cheeks.

And even more wonderful,
I can see Faith, lying in the bed,
    her
    eyes
    open.

Emma's dad bends down and
    helps me pick up
    the flowers.

    We almost lost Faith last night, he says, handing me
    black-eyed Susans and asters, *but she came back to us.*

FAITH

They say
I nearly
died.
Twice.
Once in
surgery,
and again
last night.
And I know
it's true.
Because of
the birds,
and because
of the voices
calling me
back.

Especially
Emma's.
Her voice
was the
loudest.

And it
makes sense,
because
after all,
I've

never been
able to
say
no
to
Emma.

MAXIE

For everyone else
school started
a week ago,
but I finally go to school
ten days after
    that night.

I don't want to
but Mom keeps saying it's best
to try to stick to a routine,
to keep things
the way they were
    before
    it happened.

As if that was even
    possible.

And it sucks.
The minute I walk through the doors,
    I know I can't be
    there.

It was already going
to be weird,
as new/old girl.

But because of
what happened
it is like I have this
giant RED letter
pinned
to my chest.

Except I don't know
what letter
it is.
No one does.
So I either get these
sad,
pitying looks,
or else eyes that
dart away.
Like looking at me
might get them
        shot, too.

Emma, and Faith,
and Felix
are all still in
the hospital.
And, weirdly, the silence about
Brendan
continues.
No one knows what happened
to him, even
        where he is.

It's like he's surrounded
by this
cloud of secrecy.
Even all those reporters
can't find out the truth.

Chloe and Anil
have friends
who circle them
protectively
like wagon trains
in the
        Old West.

I see Anil once,
coming out of math.
He calls out,
but I run,
in the other direction.
        Pathetic.
        Cowardly.

I can't talk to Anil.
If I did,
if I looked into his eyes,
the tears
would start up again
        and
        not
        stop.

Hiding behind my
locker door, I overhear Chloe,
pale, foot in a boot,
leaning on crutches,
talking to her friends.

> *No, I wasn't shot,* she says. *I just tripped and cut my*
> *foot. You guys know what a klutz I am.*

Her friends laugh
and hug her.

And I start to feel sorry for myself
because I am the new/old girl,
who nobody really knows,
nobody hugs.

Then I notice two girls whispering,
pointing at me,
not with their fingers,
but with their eyes.

I turn and run
down the hall
and don't stop
until I get
      home.

CHLOE

"Before Ghosting and After Ghosting"

Bad:

Twenty stitches
and a foot I can't walk on
for a week.

No more Anil.
(His parents
won't let him see
me,
or any of us
who were there
that night.)

My mother freaking out
all over me,
all the time.
At first I wanted her
warm, comforting hugs,
but by the second week,
oh my god.

Reporters,
especially the one
with the flippy,
fake blonde hair

who asked if I felt guilty
because I suggested ghosting
in the first place.
Mom stepped in then
and blasted her.

And one more thing:
Nightmares.
Every night.

Good:
Dad flew in from California.
Yeah, without his new little family.
That was a hug
I'll remember for
a <u>long</u> time.

Teachers are a lot nicer.
Mr. Chandler even gave me
an A I didn't deserve
on the first paper I wrote
after ghosting.

Oh, and Josh called.
A lot.

FAITH

The doctors
say I lost
a dangerous
amount
of blood.
That I
should
have died.

I sleep
most of
the time.
And when
I wake up
Mom or
Dad or
a nurse is
usually
there,
but once
no one
is there
and panic
flutters
in my chest
like it's
suddenly
filled with

those
white birds.

But then
I look
over at
the tray
table
next to
me, and
someone
has set
a small
folded
paper
crane,
a gleaming
white one,
right there
beside me.
The fluttery
feeling
eases and
I smile.

Then
another
time when
I wake up,
I open my
eyes to see

not just the
one white
paper crane
but dozens
of them,
all over
the room.

My mom
tells me
that my
friends from
school made
them and
that each
one has
a poem
folded inside.

I'm grateful
and astounded
that my
friends
somehow
knew about
the white birds
even though
I haven't
told a
single
soul.

ANIL

1. It has been three weeks
   since that night
   and today my mother
   has spent the whole day
   in the kitchen.

   She is preparing a
   traditional Indian feast.
   She says it's in honor of
   Ganesh Chaturthi,
   the celebration of the
   birthday of Lord Ganesha,
   son of Shiva and Parvati,
   whose head was sliced off
   by Shiva during a fierce
   battle of the gods
   and replaced with
   a baby elephant's.
   Ganesha is the god of
   wisdom, prosperity,
   and good fortune.

   I looked online and
   discovered that
   Ganesh Chaturthi was
   a week ago.

I think my mother is
worried that I am not
eating enough.

2. The smell of the food
    fills the house,
    stirring my appetite,
    and when I speak on the
    phone with Viraj, who has been
    calling more often than usual,
    he claims he can even smell it
    in Boston. And he makes a gagging sound.
    But I love the deep rich smell of
    Indian cooking.

    It is pungent and tangible and I
    welcome the distraction
    and comfort of it.

3. My mother made my favorite,
    red lentils and rice,
    but there are
    also *kudumulu*,
    steamed rice flour dumplings
    with coconut stuffing.
    She also prepared six varieties
    of *naivedyam*,
    my favorite of which is
    balehannu rasayana,
    a banana fruit salad.

My mother even dug up
a plaster of paris statue of
the potbellied,
elephant-headed Ganesha,
which she put in the center
of the table.

4. After dinner I lie on my bed,
    stomach full,
    looking up at those
    glow-in-the-dark stars.

    And then,
    not for the first time,
    or the last,
    I think about
    Maxie.

CHLOE

"The Break"

After that night
the seven of us who were there
all spin off in different directions.
It reminds me of the "break" in billiards,
which I learned about from Josh,
who plays a lot of pool.

Like the "break"
this is how we all spun off:

> Brendan disappears.
> Felix is in a coma.
> Emma is always away somewhere for surgery.
> Maxie no one ever sees, like she's exiled herself.
> Anil's parents don't let him hang out with any of us,
> > especially me.

And I guess that makes
the kid with the gun,
Walter Smith,
the cue ball.

MAXIE

This strange thing
starts to happen.
I hear little whispers of it
here and there,
but then it picks up steam.

The best way I can
describe it is that
a "cult of Chloe"
begins to form.

It starts after Anil writes
the article for the school paper
about
       that night.

I heard he did it
because he was
fed up
with all the
half-truths
and the
controversy.

And it was good he did.
Because the stories that had been
swirling around

were freakish, scary.
Not that what happened
wasn't
freakish.
Scary.

It was.

But not:
>   that we came upon
>   Walter Smith eviscerating
>   a dead crow,
or
>   that he stuck a gun in Emma's
>   mouth and made her beg
>   for her life.

But when everyone learns
how Chloe got the shooter
to give her
the gun,
well, that did it.
The story spread like wildfire
and Chloe was all anyone could
talk about.

ANIL

1. There were a lot of rumors
   going around,
   so I decided to tell
   what really happened,
   the truth, as I saw it,
   which is:

2. We were in the SUV,
   Chloe and Maxie and I,
   with Felix,
   who had lost
   consciousness.
   I had taken over from Chloe,
   keeping up the
   pressure on the
   makeshift, blood-soaked bandage
   and Maxie was holding Felix's hand,
   telling him to hang on
   and that he'd be all right.

   Then some noise or movement
   from outside the car
   made all three of us
   look up at the same time,
   and we saw, and heard,
   the final gunshot,
   saw Brendan and Emma go down.

There was a horrible moment
of silence, then Maxie
let out a gasping sound
and a stricken whispered *oh no please God.*

We stared out at the shooter,
who was still holding the rifle,
standing very still,
gazing down at the bodies
lying on the ground.
I remember thinking how small
he looked. Like a boy.
Then I heard
Chloe let out a sigh.

She slid through the half-open car door
and hobbled across the grass,
her right foot slipping around
in her bloody sandal.

The shooter didn't move,
just watched her
coming toward him.

3. She stopped a couple of feet
    away from him
    and held out her hand.
    I swear she looked like some
    unearthly angel-madonna.
    After a few seconds,

the shooter handed her
the rifle.
Just like that.

She looked down at the gun,
like she didn't know
what to do with it.
Then she threw it away.

The rifle skittered
across the sidewalk
with a harsh, clattering sound,
then came to a stop.

4.   Sirens were getting louder
and the shooter,
the small kid in a baggy green sweatshirt,
suddenly sat down
on the curb
and started to cry.

Chloe crossed over
and sat next to him.

When the first ambulance arrived,
with a police car right behind it,
she was still there.
Sitting beside him.

CHLOE

"Reasons We Do Things"

I don't really know
why I did it.
He just looked so pathetic,
this skinny little guy
who'd hurt all these people
and didn't seem to understand
any of it.

And all of a sudden
I got fed up.
Someone needed
to take that stupid gun
away from him
before anyone
else got shot.

I guess he could have shot me, too,
but I didn't really think about it,
not then.
Which was dumb.

Except this time
it turns out
I was dumb
<u>and</u>
I was smart.

POLICE CHIEF AUBREY DELAFIELD

Walter Smith was denied bail,
which was no surprise.
I attended the hearing
and the kid looked like a ghost,
paste-white pale,
and like he had no clue
where he was.

When I realized he was headed for
Cook County Jail, I knew Walter Smith
would be eaten alive.
So I put in a word,
to see if there was any way
to keep him sequestered.
Turned out he was on suicide watch
so they put him in solitary.
And kept him there.

Even now, a month later,
gawkers still drive by the house,
but there's nothing to see.
The house is deserted.

A distant cousin came
and put Adeline in an assisted-care facility.

We had the photos printed up,

the ones Maxine Kalman took that night.
There's one of those two girls,
their smiling faces lit up
by the light of their cell phones.

And when I think of what came after,
   the sidewalk slick with blood,
   the ambulances,
   the havoc done to so many lives,
the memory of those smiling faces
knocks me flat.
It's an image
that will stay burned
in my mind.
Forever.

CHLOE

"How Much It Sucks to Be a Cult Leader"

The cult thing
freaked me out.

I mean, it seemed so stupid.
Freshman girls
        following me around.
The hockey goalie
        who brought me flowers
        every day for a week.
Little pieces of candy
        stuffed into my locker.

Even Josh began to bug me,
being so nice all the time.
It seemed fake.
I mean, it made no sense.
None of it had <u>anything</u> to do with what
really happened
that night.

It got so I didn't want
to go to school,
but Mom made me.
She said it would
die down eventually.

Which it did,
finally.

During the worst of it
I started going
to the hospital
every day after school.
I liked being there.
I liked the smell of it,
which I know sounds weird.

This one orderly,
a guy with dreads
and a friendly, jokey manner,
asked me why I was there
all the time
so I told him.

He suggested I might want
to volunteer.
There are kids
from the high school,
he said
who volunteer here.
Nothing too glamorous,
but since you like it here,
might as well put you
to work.

He sent me to a lady

who said she could fix me up
with about seven hours a week.

I think that orderly
with the dreads
put in a good word for me,
plus, let's face it,
everyone at the hospital
knew I was one of
"those kids."

ANIL

1. I didn't set out to
   build a shrine.
   It just sort of
   happened.

   It started the morning after
   that night
   when I placed the pop-top from
   the can of MoonBuzz
   on my dresser.
   I had pried it off while I was talking
   to Maxie and Felix,
   a nervous habit I have.
   Must've slipped it in my pocket
   when I went into the party.

   That afternoon
   I added a small splinter of glass,
   a shattered bit of windshield,
   which I found lodged under a flap
   of my cargo shorts.

2. The third thing I added
   was also glass,
   a piece of sea glass.
   I found it in a jar in our basement,
   where we put all the shells
   we've collected on family trips to Florida.

I don't remember which trip,
or which of us found it,
but it was a pale, frosty green
and it made me think of Maxie.

3. Then I added a candle
to represent the
vigil I didn't attend.

4. And then a rose.
Because of the roses
in the pots that Chloe broke.
I read about them in the newspaper.
In an article about
the grandmother of the shooter
and about the roses she loved so much.

5. My mother noticed my shrine.
And she understood right away.

It's your ghar mandir, she said.

She told me that in India
people build *ghar mandirs*
in their homes,
and each morning
they sit before them,
to still their minds.
To pray.

It will help you heal, she said.

6.   My dad says nothing about the shrine,
though he must notice it
every time he comes into my room.

I am at my desk,
doing chemistry homework
when he knocks
and opens the door a crack.

Anil, he says. *A word?*

I nod and set down my pen.

I just wanted to tell you, he says, and his words are
halting, not smooth the way he usually speaks,
just how . . . proud I am of you.

I say nothing, surprised.

*I spoke to a colleague the other day who knows one
of the EMT responders who was on the scene that
night, and he said that what you did, the way you
reacted, in very extreme circumstances, your quick
thinking, probably saved Felix Jones's life.*

I shake my head.

It wasn't anything. I just . . . , I say.

My father raises his hand
to stop me.

Not everyone could have done what you did, son,
he said. *I know you have had your doubts, but I
must say this to you now. You have the heart of a
doctor. That is all.*

And he turns to leave.
I watch him go out the door,
shutting it carefully
behind him,
and part of me is angry,
with the feeling that he is using
this thing that happened,
this nightmarish,
tragic thing
that will haunt me
for the rest of my life,
to point me in the direction
he has always wanted me to go.

But part of me, I confess,
thinks that just maybe he's right.
And I discover,
with a sense of wonder,
that it makes me
happy.

MAXIE

One day at the drugstore
I hear two ladies talking.

> *. . . drunk, trespassing,* one says. *Well, I'm sorry but I*
> *think those kids got what they deserved.*

And I immediately know what kids
she's talking about.
Us kids.

And I wonder,
is she right?

Did
    Felix,
    Emma,
    Faith,
    all of us—
    even the boy Walter Smith—
did we get
what we
deserved?

CHLOE

"The Blame Game"

Everyone had an opinion
whose fault it was.
Everyone.

Mom's Aunt Marceline.
My dentist.
The checkout girl at Dominick's.
The substitute gym teacher with the freakishly large
earlobes.

And one thing I've learned is
people aren't shy about giving
their opinion.

Here's my tally on how it fell out:

1. *Brendan, for shooting off that stupid gun*
2. *Emma, for suggesting we go to the "ghost house"*
3. *Me, for bringing up ghosting in the first place and for
   being a klutz and breaking the flowerpots.*
4. *Anil, Maxie, and Felix, for not speaking up about the
   gun in the glove compartment*
5. *All of us, for drinking MoonBuzz*

So, yeah, I think about it a lot.
And yeah, I wish I'd kept my mouth shut.

That we'd gone to a 3-D movie instead.
But the truth is, blaming isn't going to
change one single thing.

And that's exactly what I said to
that substitute gym teacher
with her stupid big earlobes.

MAXIE

School is torture.
Some days I
can't even get out
of bed.

I go to a therapist
and it helps.
A little.
She says it'll
        take time.

Emma,
when she came back,
in between
all her surgeries,
wearing a perpetual cast,
tried pulling me into
her wagon train
        of friends.

I was grateful at first,
felt a little less lonely,
but then I started feeling
even lonelier than before.
Because it was obvious to me
that Emma's friends
        wished I wasn't there.

So I started avoiding Emma.
Went back to avoiding everyone,
including Anil.
Especially Anil.
Which is ironic since one of
the few things that
keeps me from crying
is remembering
his story about
the two telescopes.

ANIL

1.   I think about Maxie a lot,
worry about her.

In the first few weeks after
that night
it seemed like I never saw her
around school,
to the point that
I even wondered if her parents
had decided to switch her to
another school.

Then I'd catch a glimpse of her.
But she always stayed far away.
Like she couldn't bear
the sight of me.

MAXIE

There was a story
printed in the Chicago paper
saying that,
back when he was in middle school,
Walter Smith
had
stabbed
a teacher
in the neck
with a pencil.

That's when his grandmother
pulled him out of school
and started
homeschooling him.

But it turned out to be
another kid entirely,
a kid whose name wasn't even
Walter,
and who went to a
different
middle school.

I found myself
feeling disappointed,
    wishing it were true.

Because then I could see
Walter Smith
as a
neck-stabbing monster,
not the pathetic boy
in too-big glasses
who couldn't stop
        crying.

Like me.

ANIL

1. I visit Felix sometimes
   at the hospital,
   just sit by his bed,
   listen to the machines
   that keep him alive.

   I even talk to him,
   though at first it felt awkward.
   But research shows that people in a coma
   really do hear what you're saying.

   Once I talked to him about Maxie.
   How even though I hadn't met her
   until that night,
   I miss her in this bottomless way,
   as if I had known her
   my whole life.

   And then one afternoon
   when I get to Felix's room
   Maxie is sitting by his bed,
   reading him a book.

   I watch her face,
   her lips moving.
   And suddenly,
   it's like I've turned into

a slab of granite,
completely unable to move
or speak.

I'm reminded of what my mother
once told me about snake charmers in India,
with those cobras in a basket,
who seem to be hypnotized
by the music of the flute.
But it turns out that cobras,
all snakes in fact,
are mostly deaf.
The only way they can hear is through vibrations
in their jawbones
and flute playing doesn't send out
a ton of vibrations.

So scientists figured out that it wasn't the music
that hypnotizes them,
but the movement of the charmer's body.
Just like it's the movement of Maxie's lips
that has me transfixed.

My mother also told me that,
for obvious reasons,
snake charmers will often either
defang their snakes
or sew their mouths shut,
leaving only enough room for the tongue
to slide in and out.

Hi, Maxie, I say softly, finally able to move my
own tongue.

Her head jerks around
and she almost drops the book.
But like at school,
she won't even
look at me.

I have to go, she says to Felix, knowing I'm the
only one who can hear her.

2.   Maxie hurries out of the room,
     eyes down.
     I watch her go,
     helpless as a snake with its
     mouth sewn shut.

MAXIE

One Saturday night
Emma ambushes me.

She shows up at my door
on crutches,
carrying a stack
of DVDs
and popcorn.

Before I can react
she is on my couch,
TV remote in
her hand.

> *Come on in,* I say, still standing by the front door.
> *Yeah, well, thing is, Maxie,* Emma says, *I hear you're
> like a total recluse. And me, I'm sick of my friends
> being so fake nice all the time. And I know all they
> want to do is get back to normal, go out, and get
> drunk on a Saturday night. So I thought maybe you
> and I could hang out.*

I look at her, my arms crossed
over my chest.

> *We don't have to talk,* Emma says.

Okay, I say, and sit beside her on the couch. *What'd
you bring?*

So we settle back,
eat popcorn,
and watch a movie
about time travel.
We don't talk.

It isn't until the movie's over
and she's getting ready to go,
that I blurt out,

Have you seen Brendan?

She doesn't speak,
just stands there
leaning on
her crutches.
The silence hangs
between us.

No, she says finally.
Do you know anything, how he is?
No, she says again, her voice flat. *And yes, I've heard
  the rumors, too, that he's brain dead in some
  Chicago hospital.*

Her eyes suddenly fill
with tears.

I start to go to her,
to hug her,
but she puts up a hand
to hold me away.

I'm fine, she says.

But she isn't.
And how could she be?
Whatever's happened to Brendan
happened because he was
trying to
     save her life.

CHLOE

"Spirit Week"

Before ghosting I loved Spirit Week,
the whole gung-ho, rah rah,
support-your-school thing.
Coming up with silly, over-the-top outfits
while still trying to look cute.

But when I get the schedule
for this year's Spirit Week
I feel sick to my stomach.

> MONDAY—Tie-dye
> TUESDAY—Rock band/Concert T-shirts
> WEDNESDAY—Patriotic
> THURSDAY—School Pride (scarlet and yellow)
> FRIDAY—yellow ribbons to honor shooting victims

I mean that's great,
everyone showing their sympathy and support,
but what good are a bunch of cheap little yellow ribbons
going to do for
Faith,
Emma,
Felix,
and
Brendan?

MAXIE

Poor Rita Bell.
Rita,
    cheerleading captain,
    vice president of student council,
    queen of community service,
not to mention
    friendly green eyes,
    tumbling black curls,
    wide smile,
    whitest teeth.

In a normal year,
a year with
no ghosting,
no Walter Smith,
Rita would've been
a shoo-in for
Homecoming Queen.

Sure, Emma and Chloe
would've come close,
but no more than second and third,
probably in that order.

But because of
that night,

poor Rita
comes in a distant third.

Even though Emma
told everyone <u>not</u> to
vote for her
since she wouldn't even
be in town for Homecoming,
a third surgery,
in Boston this time,
she comes in
second anyway.

It's Chloe
who is crowned
Homecoming Queen.
By a landslide.

And she looks luminous,
a simple white dress,
her honey-colored hair
hanging loose,
her face pale,
standing beside
        the Homecoming King.

Brendan.
In his wheelchair.

BRENDAN

Homecoming King.
What a fucking joke.

I wave to all the faceless,
clueless people in the stands.

Then my eyes light on Bobby,
sitting in the front row, between our parents.

He's got this huge smile, beaming like I'm
some kind of hero. And that's what I am, right?

The guy who stepped between Emma
and a bullet. Except for one thing.

I'm <u>also</u> the asshole who fired off Daddy's gun
and got us shot, maimed, almost killed.

But hell, in this country
we like our messed-up heroes.

So here I sit in my wheelchair,
Homecoming King.

Got my khakis, button-down shirt,
red tie, hair neatly combed.

Right smack dab in the middle of the field

I used to play lacrosse on.

But it doesn't matter,
none of it fucking matters.

Then Chloe leans down
and whispers soft in my ear.

This sucks, doesn't it?

I look up at her in surprise.

Yes, I say. *It sucks.*

EMMA

If someone takes a bullet for you,
saves your life,
what do you owe them?

Everything?

Or the truth?

BRENDAN

I'll never forget the moment
when my dad realized.

When the last expensive doctor
spelled it out for us in black and white.

That no amount of money,
no number of pulled strings,

no browbeating or foot stomping,
yelling or bullying,

that no ramped-up brand of positive thinking
would get him a son with legs that worked.

We were sitting in the office of the best orthopedic
surgeon in the United States of America.

I am very sorry to have to tell you, Brendan,
Mr. Donnelly, Dr. Wyamussing said, looking at each
of us in turn, *but there is nothing that can be done to*
reverse the paralysis.

My dad went all quiet.
Then the doctor's pager beeped.

Sorry, I have to take this, Dr. Wyamussing said, after a
quick look at the pager. *Take however long you need.*

I can't say it was a big shock.
I think I knew it that first moment.

When I woke up in the hospital
and couldn't feel my legs.

But the finality of the doctor's words,
the cold, hard fact

that I would never walk, run,
play lacrosse, swim, ski,

that I would never do
any of the things you do with legs . . .

Well, it gave me this sick, frozen feeling
that made it hard to breathe.

Okay, Dad says. *So now we know.*

I had closed my eyes,
and was taking deep breaths.

I felt his hand on my shoulder
and opened my eyes.

His eyes were bright,
almost as if there were tears in them.

But he was also wearing this
wide, manic smile.

What do the Donnellys do with lemons, son? he said.

I stared back at him, my entire body feeling
as if it had turned to ice.

Make fucking lemonade, I said.
That's my boy, he said.

FAITH

It has
been
almost
two months
since
that night.

Front stoops
in the
neighborhood
are dotted
with orange
pumpkins,
and ghosts
made of white
bedsheets
hang from
tree limbs,
fluttering
in the autumn
wind.

We've
just
finished
dinner,
and Emma

and I have
hobbled out
to the
backyard
with Polly.

It is one
of those
mild nights
you sometimes
get in
mid-October,
and we're
lying,
side by side,
on the
hammock,
with our
matching casts
on our
right legs.

I mean,
what are
the odds that
two sisters
would have
fractured
bones
in the
same leg?

One from
jumping out
of a car
and
the other
from
a bullet.

Turns out
Emma's was more
complicated,
fractured in
three places.
Mine was a
cleaner break,
but the scar
on my leg
is ugly,
a great
puckered
dent in
my thigh.

They said
that I
can have
plastic surgery
later,
which will
make it look
a lot better.

Emma likes
to tease me,
calling me a
psycho nutjob
for setting out
that night
on my bike
to save
our family.

I don't mind
her teasing.
In fact,
I call her a
psycho nutjob
right back
for jumping
out of a
speeding car.

We have this
running joke
about which
one of us
got it worse.

And tonight
on the
hammock,
we start up
again.

Okay, Polly, you decide, Emma finally says, reaching
over and rubbing Polly's ears.

And Polly
looks from
me to Emma
as we make
our case.

I came this close to dying, I say, holding up my thumb
and forefinger with barely a sliver of space between
them. *Twice.*
I'm gonna need at least three more surgeries,
Emma says.
*I'm gonna need one more, plus I got a cracked skull and
a burr hole,* I say.
I got a concussion, Emma says.
I've got four pins in my leg, I say.
I've got five pins and three screws, Emma says.
My thigh looks like one of those sinkholes in Florida,
I say, *plus I lost twenty percent of my blood.*
*No more soccer scholarship at Penn for me, plus I may
never play soccer again,* says Emma.

I look
sideways
at her.

That's bull, I say, *I mean about never playing
soccer again.*
We'll see, she says looking up at the night sky.

Polly barks
then,
and lays
her head
on Emma's
thigh.

See, I win! Emma laughs.
Still the same old Emma, I say, grinning at her.

Her smile
fades.

No, she says. *Not the same old Emma.*

EMMA

One thing that's happened is
I think a lot about death.
I never used to, but now I do.

Faith told me about the white birds
and the quiet, peaceful feeling
she got when she almost died.

I felt jealous when she told me.
And I find myself wondering if it's
different for each person.

Maybe someone good and true like Faith
is worthy of the quiet and the white birds.
But someone like me, not so much.

Because all of it—Brendan in a wheelchair,
Felix in a coma, Faith almost dying
is my fault.

I've always careened through my life,
full speed, doing exactly what I want,
without thinking about the consequences.

And see what happened.
So I think about death
and I keep wondering:

Is it really white birds and quiet?
Or maybe it's a dark hole
you get sucked into.

Or a place of fire.
Or maybe it's just
nothing.

The scary thing is that
these days
nothing actually sounds good.

FAITH

One day,
eating
peanut butter
sandwiches
in the kitchen,
I tell Emma
how floored
I am by
my friends,
how amazing
they've been,
all those
paper cranes.

> *You deserve it,* she says. *That girl Francesca, the*
> *one with the tattoo on her ankle, she's the one who*
> *organized it all, right?*
> *Yeah,* I say.

Emma hobbles
to the fridge
for more milk.

> *Em,* I blurt, *what's going on with you and Brendan?*

Her back
gets stiff.

Then she
turns to me.

I . . . I don't know, Faith, she says, her face sad. *And that's the truth. I've seen him a couple times and he acts the same, like nothing's happened, nothing's wrong. But it's all on the surface, with lots of jokes about the wheelchair, like he doesn't care.*

She comes
back to
the table.

I don't even know if I'm his girlfriend anymore,
     she says.
Do you want to be? I ask.

Tears come
into her
eyes.

Oh, Faith . . . The thing is, and this sounds like bullshit now, but I'd been planning to break up with him, once school started. But now . . .

And she
starts crying.

I pull my
chair next
to hers

and put
my arms
around her.

It'll be all right, I say.

She shakes
her head.

I don't see how, she says.

And the
hopelessness
in her voice
scares me.

BRENDAN

The worst times are when
I realize I can't do something.

And people around me
try to do it for me.

I even yelled at Bobby once for that,
which made me feel like shit afterward.

Getting the car with hand controls
made a big difference.

I mastered it pretty quick
and right away felt more independent.

And I'm still good at faking most people out,
in order to get what I want.

The main thing I want right now is to numb the pain
and I figured out a good way to do that.

The only other thing
I care about is Bobby.

Don't want him freaked out by
his crippled big brother.

So he's my first passenger
in the new nifty handicapped car.

I can feel him watching me closely
as I work the hand controls.

I take him to his favorite fast-food place,
drive-through, which is a godsend for crips.

We sit in the car, munching french fries.
And it feels good.

> *I wanted to go to the hospital,* Bobby says suddenly.
> *It's okay,* I start to say, but he interrupts.
> *Dad didn't let me.*

I think about that.
And I guess Dad was protecting Bobby.

Which could be the one thing
that he and I agree about.

> *I think Dad was hoping he could make me better before*
>   *you saw me,* I say. *But it turned out he couldn't.*
> *But you're going to be okay, right?* Bobby asks.
> *Yeah,* I say, with a reassuring grin. *Not exactly what I*
>   *was planning. But I'm good.*
> *Are you still going to college?*
> *Dunno,* I say. *You need some more fries?*
> He shakes his head. *I heard you tell your girlfriend*
>   *once that you really wanted to go to college in Colorado.*

You did? I ask, surprised.
Yeah, he says, *and I think you still should, even if you
can't ski anymore.*

I reach for his fries.

'Sides, Bobby says, persistent as ever, *I looked it
up on the Internet and there is some way people in
wheelchairs can still ski.*

I feel some weird lump in my throat,
like I may throw up or cry.

That's bullshit, I say, my voice coming out rough and
angry.

Bobby shuts his mouth then,
looking at me with a confused expression.

I swallow hard,
trying to dislodge the lump.

*I'm sorry, Bobby. It's just that sometimes I get tired of
all the pretending,* I say.
I wasn't, he protests. *I did see it on the Internet.*
I'm sure you did, I say, feeling suddenly exhausted.
So, he says, his words halting, *does this mean you
won't be taking me ice-skating this winter?*

Before, when I wasn't in this chair,
ice-skating was one of our favorite things to do.

We'd go every winter,
just the two of us.

No, I mean, yes, of course, I'll take you ice-skating, I
say, forcing enthusiasm I don't feel. *Are you kidding.? I
wouldn't miss it.*

His face lights up and we high-five,
me with a big fake smile on my face.

Like I've just made a promise
I intend to keep.

MAXIE

Ever since
that night
I've been going to
the hospital,
regularly,
    to visit Felix.

Still in a coma,
hooked up to machines.
    I sit by his bed
    and read to him.

Felix's mom is there a lot.
She's very friendly,
likes to chat,
and I learn that
Felix's dad came home
from Afghanistan
right after the shooting.
But then he went back
when it looked like
Felix wasn't going to wake up
    soon.

She says he had to go
because they need the money.

She's had to quit her job
to be with Felix.

But she seems okay,
strong even.
Not the depressed mom from before
who couldn't get her act together
        to pay bills
        and cook meals.

Now she's more like the mom
I remember from when we were
kids.

When his mom isn't there
I read to Felix.

At first I read him
random things,
like homework
assignments, but then
I remember
those Joey Pigza books,
his favorites
from 5th grade.

I get all four books
from the library
and after I finish
the first one,
I decide to read them

all straight through.
And I begin to have this
superstitious belief
that Felix will wake up
when I come to
    the last word of
    the last book.

I get my hopes up
way too high.
And keep looking at him
after practically every sentence
during that last chapter.

But he doesn't
wake up.
The machines just keep
whirring.

So I pick up the very first book
and start over,
from the beginning.

EMMA

One afternoon I go to
visit Brendan and he is
playing a video game.

It's the kind where you
track people down
and shoot them.

I can't believe he'd want to play
a game like that, not after
that night.

Seeing the splattered blood,
hearing the muted death cries,
makes me feel sick.

I struggle to tune it out,
cold sweat prickling my skin.
I ask how his Thanksgiving was.

> *It was okay,* he says. *Though I passed when it came to
> the whole what-have-we-got-to-be-thankful-for routine.
> For obvious reasons.* Patting the arm of his wheelchair,
> he gives me a sweet, dimpled smile.

Then he blasts a guy in a tan raincoat
and blood fountains out onto the sidewalk.

My breathing gets ragged. I want to go.

But I find myself wondering;
is Brendan imagining that each of these
guys he's blowing away is Walter Smith?

Before that night I would have asked him,
I would have made him tell me
what's really going on with him.

But I can't now. And I don't know why,
except I think it's because I'm afraid,
afraid of what I'll hear.

Brendan sets down
the game controller and
wheels himself around to face me.

> *So, Emma,* he says, looking me straight in the eye,
> *it's really nice of you to make the effort to come see me.*
> *It's more than a lot of kids have done. And I do really*
> *appreciate it and all. But I've been thinking, it'd be*
> *better for me, if you didn't, anymore.*

I stare at him.

> *I'm sorry to be so blunt, but I . . . I mean I guess it's just*
> *   not working anymore. Guess I need time.*
> *Okay,* I mumble, *if that's how you feel.*
> *It is,* he says, picking up the controller again.
> *Brendan,* I blurt out, *are you okay?*

Which, the minute I say it,
sounds so unbelievably
lame.

He looks at me,
and his mouth twists up into
a smile.

And for a minute I see something dark,
a deep black rage,
underneath that smile.

Then he just turns back to his video game
and blasts some guy in a cowboy hat
to hell.

MAXIE

It's a quiet Thursday afternoon
and it must be somebody's birthday
because a couple of
Mylar balloons are bobbing
over the nurses' station.

And a dark-haired nurse
gives me a cheery smile
as I walk by.

Felix looks the same as usual,
the right side of his face
swathed in gauze,
covering his
missing eye.

The machines are whirring away,
the IV bottle doing its continual
        dripping thing.

I sit down,
staring at the steady
rise and fall
of his chest,
and suddenly I am
        overcome with
        sadness.

What if Felix
      never
            wakes up?

Tears prick at my eyes
and, determined not
to cry,
I pick up Joey Pigza,
and start where I left off
the day before.

Then I come to
one of my favorite bits,
when Joey Pigza's dad talks
about the bad stuff he
did in the past when
he was
      drinking
      too much.

Joey's dad says, *"My past. . . gets sort of scary and ugly
and to tell you the truth I'd just rather have, you know,
the new times to talk about. The now times. I'd rather
just show you Storybook Land and play baseball and
work on making new memories."*

And I can't help thinking about
my dad
and his beers this summer and
also about
Felix's dad

and what he did to Felix's mom,
and then about MoonBuzz and
the bad things that happened
  that night.

And I begin to start wondering
if there can ever
be any
  new now times
  to replace the
  old bad ones.

Tears come.
Blinking them back,
I take a few deep breaths
and start reading again.

But all of a sudden
I hear
  a little
  noise.

I automatically look
at the machines
hooked up to Felix
to see if something is
wrong,
but they're all
humming along,
same as usual.
Then I look at Felix

and his eyelid,
the one that isn't
covered with bandages,
is
twitching
    all over
    the place,
which I've never seen
it do before.

Then the noise
comes again
and I see his mouth
move
and that the noise
is a little grunt
coming from
HIM.

My heart starts
    hammering.

Felix?

FELIX

joey pigza and i are walking down the sidewalk, past
bonnie's sweet shop, and he's bouncing along, like a
springy crazy rubber ball, like he might bounce himself
straight up to the sky.

but i pull him back down, and tell him we need to talk,
about what happened, and he turns to me, all serious, and
says he doesn't want to talk about the past.

The past is messed up, Joey, he says.

i get confused because i'm not joey, he is.

but then he's telling me about his drinking, about how
when he drinks too much he does stupid stuff. and now
i'm really confused, because he's not joey, and i'm not joey.
instead, he's my dad, or else he's joey's dad.

then he says:

I'm sorry.

and that's when i wake up.

MAXIE

Felix is really groggy
and confused,
like he has no idea
why he's in
>   the hospital.

> *Max?* he says in a hoarse raspy voice.
> *Yeah, Felix,* I say, my heart ready to burst out of
>   my chest.

I know I should be calling
the nurse,
or
Felix's mom,
but for
just this moment
I want to gaze back into
that open,
wide-awake,
no-more-coma
>   eye.

Then,
even though it's like
a line out of
a dumb movie,
I can't help myself

and say,
with a big, beaming
    smile on my face,

    Welcome back, Felix.

And guess what.
Felix looks at me
and smiles.

FELIX

when i woke up my whole body ached. and my vision was weird. i couldn't figure out for a while that it was because my right eye was gone.

mom went nuts when she came in the hospital room and saw i was awake. and max's smile couldn't have been any wider. so even though my body felt weak and useless, like all my muscles had been vaporized, it still felt good, to be back.

here's the amazing thing, though. i have no memory of that night. zero. zilch.

i remember getting high in the suv outside that party, hearing anil's telescope story and max talking about her day at the beach with the sea glass and sandcastle. but after that, nothing.

mom and the doctors didn't tell me right away what happened. just said there had been an accident. i assumed it was a car accident. but when i got stronger, when i wasn't so freaked out about my eye, mom told me the whole story.

it was unreal. didn't even sound familiar, or like it could actually be true. i mean, i believed her. i had to. but faith almost dying, brendan in a wheelchair, and a guy named walter smith in jail awaiting trial, i couldn't wrap my mind around it.

the doctors said that my amnesia about that night was completely to be expected. and that most likely i'd never remember any of it. it kind of bothered me to have this big fairly crucial chunk of my life be missing, along with my eye. but max said i was lucky.

max even said she'd give anything to have that night wiped from her memory, forever. and seeing the pain in her face, i realized that maybe i am lucky.

at least about that.

CHLOE

"One Thing I Wish I Hadn't Seen"

When I'm doing
my volunteer shift
at the hospital
sometimes I spot
Brendan in his wheelchair,
arriving for, or leaving after,
outpatient rehab.

One day I see him chatting up
Suzie, this cute young nurse
with curly brown hair.

They're laughing
and flirting and
I'm thinking it's really nice
to see Brendan smiling
like that, but then I see her
slip him something that
looks like pills.

The way she darts her
eyes around to see if
anyone is watching
makes me wonder

FAITH

I dream
sometimes
about those
white birds
and in
the dream
they begin
to form
into wings
around my
shoulders,
a giant
pair of wings
made up
of white
feathered
birds
who are
lifting me
higher and
higher.

But then
I hear voices
from below,
calling me.

Faith, they say. *Come back.*

And it's
Emma's voice,
loudest
of course,
and Dad's
and Mom's,
even Polly
has a voice
in this
dream.

So I tell
the birds
that I need to
go back.

And gently,
very gently,
they start to
descend,
back down
to
earth.

I told
my friend
Francesca
about
that dream
and she
teased me

about my
Near Death
Experience,
said that
Oprah will
probably
be calling
to ask for
an interview.

And then
she folded me
the most
beautiful
white
paper crane
I'd ever
seen.

EMMA

I dream about that boy Walter Smith.
Over and over I dream about him,
his rifle pointed straight at me.

But in the dream when I raise my hand,
the thing in my hand isn't a rubber crow.
It's a gun.

In the dream I aim that gun at Walter Smith,
and I shoot him. Again and again.
Bullets tearing into him. Until he is dead.

FELIX

mom tells me that the first thing she did when i came out
of the coma was to call my dad in afghanistan. she said
it took a little maneuvering but he's coming home, has a
flight out next saturday.

> *I'm not seeing him,* I say, interrupting her going on
> about how excited he was to get the news and all of
> us being together for Christmas.
> *What?* she says.
> *He never said he was sorry.*
> *What do you mean?* she asks, looking anxious.
> *He never told me he was sorry. Did he ever say he was*
> *sorry to you?*

she stares at me.

> *Felix, if you're talking about last year, that night when*
> *you saw . . . ,* she says. *I mean, it really wasn't what*
> *you thought it was.*
> *Mom,* I say, *I know exactly what it was. And it was*
> *really messed up. And it was even more messed up*
> *that you acted like nothing happened, that you're still*
> *acting like nothing happened.*

tears suddenly flood her eyes.

> *I . . . Felix, it's just . . . ,* she starts.

then she breaks down, sobbing hard, her whole body shaking. and suddenly she runs out of the room. i want to get up and follow her but i can't. more than three months on my back in a hospital bed has turned my muscles into a bunch of worn-out rubber bands. they say it's going to take at least a month of rehab for me to even be able to walk again.

i stare at the door, feeling bad. but i don't regret what i said. and i'm not going to change my mind.

MAXIE

I visit Felix
in the hospital,
a few days after he gets
his new eye,
    his fake eye.

He asked me to come because
he said he wanted to
test drive it
with me,
since I had a good eye (ha-ha)
for
color
and light.

He had told me all about
how they would fit him
for it,
how it would match his
other eye
exactly,
how it wouldn't be made of glass
like he was hoping,
but of some
    acrylic material.

When I walk in the room

Felix is sitting up in bed.
And it is amazing
to see him,
with no more bandages,
and two eyes
    looking back at me.

There is puckering
in the skin
around his right eye
and some faint white scarring,
but it really is
something,
how real
his new eye
looks.

    Wow, I say.
    Yeah, it's pretty awesome, what they can do, he says
        If you look closely, you can tell, because of the way it
        doesn't move like the other.
    If you say so. But the color is perfect. Amazing, I say.

He smiles.

    Thanks, Max, he says. *I can do tricks. Wanna see?*
    I don't know . . . , I answer, apprehensive.

And of course he does it,
pops his fake eye
right out of the

socket,
which gives me sort of a sick feeling,
    mainly because of the hollowed-in
    look of the empty socket.

But he's holding the acrylic eye
in the palm of his hand,
and I can't resist.
I pull out
    my camera.

Flash.

He beams at me.

    Nice, he says. *You should submit that to the school*
    lit magazine.
    Maybe I will, I say, smiling back.

He puts the eye back in,
and I don't watch.

    The nurses say I shouldn't do that too much, unsanitary
    or something, but I knew you'd appreciate it, Felix says.
    Do you know when you might be going home? I ask.
    I think pretty soon, he starts, but then I see him
    looking past me toward the door.

Emma is standing there,
leaning on crutches,
in the doorway.

Hey, Felix, she says with a grin, *I heard you finally woke up.*

Felix grins back.

I was just showing Max my new eye, he says.

Emma comes further into the room,
peering closely at
Felix's face.

Jeez, I can barely tell which eye is the fake one, she says.

He points to
his right eye.

Excellent, she says.
You doing okay, Emma? Felix asks.
Yeah, she says. *I'm hoping this next surgery is the last.
It's getting old.*

She spots the pile of
Joey Pigza books.

Hey, I remember those, she says, crossing over to them
and picking one up. *You read them about twenty
times, back in middle school.*
*Yeah, and did you hear about my Joey Pigza miracle?
Max was reading it to me and, shazam, I woke up,*
Felix says.

Good old Joey Pigza, she says. *Faith had a miracle, too.*
   An official NDE.
Very cool, says Felix.
Yeah, there were these white birds and glowing light . . .

While she talks
Emma has been straightening
the pile of Joey Pigza books,
but then she trails off
and suddenly looks
like she's about
to cry.

   What's wrong? I ask.
   Nothing, Emma whispers. *It's just Brendan* . . .

She stops abruptly,
an uncertain look
on her face.

The three of us get quiet.

Then Felix clears
his throat.

   Hey, Emma, I can do this amazing trick, he says.

EMMA

At first, in the weeks and months after
that night, I hated Walter Smith. I hated
everything about him. Even his name.

I hated that he took so much
from all of us, but especially
from Brendan and Felix.

But something Faith said changed me,
not right away but gradually.
She felt sorry for Walter Smith.

I was pissed when she said it,
my soft-hearted, wrongheaded
little sister.

Walter Smith was a freak,
who raised a gun to his shoulder
and tore our lives apart.

Feel sorry for him? How?
But even though I tried to avoid reading
the stories in the newspapers, I couldn't help it.

And one of them, an in-depth report
by someone who was a good writer,
told Walter Smith's life story.

And it was really sad. Walter Smith had always had
so little. Not one single person cared if he
lived or died, except his crazy old grandmother.

No mother or father or sister. No friends.
Just his cowboy books and cowboy movies.
He never had a chance.

CHLOE

*"How Many Dumb Blondes Does it Take to Screw
in a Lightbulb?"*

One of the nurses sends me
on an errand to the rehab unit
and I happen to catch Brendan
as he's finishing
his physical therapy.
I can tell he's really
working hard,
the way he used to
in lacrosse practices.
Which seems like a good sign.
Unlike that thing I saw
a while back,
with the nurse Suzie.

He's all sweaty, with a towel
draped around his neck
as he wheels toward me.

When he gets closer I can
see that his eyes are red,
the pupils constricted,
like the eyes of a patient
I helped out with last week
who had been on narcotics.

Hey, Chloe Carney, he says, *how's Highland Park
    Hospital's cutest volunteer?*
Good, I answer. And then I add, *So I saw you flirting
    with that nurse Suzie the other day.*
Oh yeah? he says, darting a little look at me.
Yeah, I say.
*What can I say? This chair is pretty much a
    chick magnet.*

He's giving me
his best dimpled smile,
but I'm not buying it.

I saw her give you pills, I say.

He looks surprised,
his smile fading a little.

Yeah, just a few sleeping pills, he says. *Sometimes I
    have trouble getting to sleep.*
I give him a steady look. *Doesn't your doctor give you
    stuff like that?*
*I ran out. Suzie was just lending a hand. Look, I won't
    do it again,* he says, flashing me that smile again.

A couple of interns in scrubs walk by.

What's she really giving you? I ask.
Huh?
*And where do you hide them, I mean from
    your parents?*

He stares up at me.
I can read the expression on his face.
It's saying, I thought
Chloe Carney was dumb.

Well? I persist.
Percocet. Under the mattress, he says.

Then he gets this look in his eyes,
like he can't believe he just
told me that.

BRENDAN

Holy crap. Why'd I do that?
Tell her?

> *It's okay,* Chloe says, putting her hand on my
> shoulder.

I shake my head.

> *What've you got, like magic powers?* I ask. *First Walter*
> *Smith and his rifle. Now me.*

Chloe Carney puts her head back
and laughs.

And I swear to God, it's one of the
nicest things I've heard in a long time.

MAXIE

After lunch one day
right before winter break,
this guy with ginger hair
comes up to me.

He wears wire-rimmed glasses
and a T-shirt that says
IF DESCARTES WAS RIGHT
YOU WOULDN'T EXIST.

You're Maxie Kalman, right? he says.
Yes, I say.
I'm Zander, editor of Versions, *the lit magazine,* he says,
    and so far, the photos I'm getting are pretty lame. So I
    was just wondering if you'd like to submit stuff.
Uh, okay, I reply, immediately thinking of the photo
    of the fake eye in Felix's hand.
Great!

Then he digs into his backpack.

Oh, and I've got some poems. Would really like to pair
    them with some cool photos. See if they inspire you, okay?

I nod, taking the
pieces of paper
he hands me.

Great, he says again. *I put my e-mail at the top there.*

Then he gives me
a big smile
and walks off.

Leaning against
my locker,
    I read the poems.

They're actually a
series of haiku,
all with the theme of
    good-bye
    or
    departure.

And they are
beautiful.

For some reason
they remind me of
    that night.

So of course,
tears come to
my eyes.

But then an
amazing thing
happens.

I say No.
Not out loud
but inside my head,
and I deliberately shift to
thinking about
those haiku and
thinking about
the photos
I could take
to capture those
beautiful words.

My tears dry,
and I feel a
tiny,
warming
glimmer of
        hopefulness.

BRENDAN

I'd been thinking about it for a long time
and decided it was time to visit Felix.

The guy who lost his eye
because of me.

Felix's house is all handicap friendly, which is a relief.
Just need to wheel myself up to the door.

His mom is surprised to see me,
but she doesn't say anything.

Felix is lying on his bed, eyes closed,
listening to an iPod.

I watch him for a few seconds,
then reach over and tap his leg.

> *Brendan, jeez,* he says, sitting up so suddenly he
> bumps his head on the headboard of his bed. *What're
> you doing here?*

I look at him closely.

> *Whoa dude, I heard you lost an eye.*
> *I did,* Felix says. He points to his right eye. *It's acrylic.*

That's freaking amazing, I say. *Think I could get some*
  acrylic legs?

He smiles, but like most of my attempts at
handicap humor it's followed by an awkward silence.

  So do you still smoke weed? I ask.
  Not so much, he says. *Kind of lost the taste for it.*
  Yeah, I know. I'm not too into drinking anymore.

I don't tell him that drinking alcohol
pretty much sucks,

since it means using the
catheter a hell of a lot more.

Plus it's much easier to pop a pill
than pour a drink when you're in a wheelchair.

  So why <u>are</u> you here? Felix asks.
  Uh, I begin, *I guess I just wanted to say that I'm sorry.*

He looks at me, shaking his head,
but I forge on.

  Yeah, I'm sorry about what happened, to you, to
  everyone. I was a dick, and if I could take back . . .

Felix interrupts me.

  Shut up, Brendan, he says. *You weren't the only one.*

We all messed up, and a bunch of stuff happened, kind
of like a chain reaction. Or one of those Rube Goldberg
contraptions.

I have no idea what the fuck
he's talking about.

My face must've showed it,
because Felix laughs.

Okay, so you remember that old board game that was
popular when we were kids, called Mouse Trap? I nod.
Well, that night was like Mouse Trap. Yeah, you were a
dick, I was too stoned, Chloe was a klutz, and Emma,
well, Emma was Emma. And then there was a crazy
dude with a shotgun.

I stare at him, then suddenly smile.

Nice. Way to sum up, I say.
Thanks, says Felix. *Feel like some guacamole?*
Sure, I say.
It's the weirdest thing, he says leading me down the
    hall. *But ever since I woke up I'm always craving*
    guacamole.

He clears a chair from the kitchen table
so I can pull my wheelchair up to it.

I watch while he halves
a couple of avocadoes.

And then he starts smashing them into a bowl,
squeezing lime into them.

He looks like a real pro, chopping jalapeños
neatly dicing a large red onion.

  It's so flipping weird to have only one eye cry, Felix
  says, wiping onion tears from his left eye.

He opens a bag of tortilla chips
and pours them into a bowl.

  My parents are getting divorced, Felix says out
  of the blue.

I don't know what to say.

  That's a bummer, I finally manage.
  Actually, no, it's a good thing, he says. *My dad is pretty*
   fucked up.
  Been there, I say.
  Yeah, I know, he says.

He pushes the bowls of guacamole
and chips toward me.

I take a big scoop
and stuff it in my mouth.

  Holy shit, this is great, I say.

I take another big mouthful
and smile.

> *Best damn guac I've had,* I say. *You should open*
> *a restaurant.*
> *Maybe I will,* he says. *I'll call it One Eye Cry.*
> *Excellent,* I say.

CHLOE

"And the Question Is: Why Do I Care?"

My dad has been calling me
a lot more regularly, which is
really nice.

He even invited me to California
for spring break
which seems like a long way away,
but I'm psyched.
He also texted me a picture
of my little half sister,
who is actually really cute,
and said she's excited to meet me.

He asks a lot about working
at the hospital. And I tell him stories,
like the one about an old lady
named Iris who's so sweet,
but usually thinks I'm either
her daughter or Hillary Clinton.
I mean, Hillary? She might, at least,
think I'm Chelsea. Which makes Dad laugh,
and then I couldn't believe it,
but out of the blue he suggests
that I think about applying to nursing school,
instead of Illinois State.

That he thinks I'm smart
enough to go to nursing school
pretty much blows my mind.

Then I tell him about this friend
of mine who I'm not that close to
but who I'm worried about,
worried that he might be
abusing drugs.
So my dad asks a few questions
And gives me some advice.
Mostly it helps just to talk about it
with someone.

But I'm still worried.

BRENDAN

I'm in my room, at my desk,
trying to concentrate on homework.

All my teachers came up with packets of stuff,
so I can graduate in June.

Math I can do, straightforward, uncomplicated.
But it'll be a miracle if I pass English.

What am I saying? It's not like anyone is
actually going to fail the crip in the wheelchair.

There's a knock at the door
but before I can say anything,

Dad walks right in.
He's got a piece of paper in his hand.

> *Good news, son,* he says. *Just heard from Sanford
> Weems, my buddy on the board at Princeton. Says here
> that as long as you can muster a 3.5, you have a decent
> chance of getting in.*

I stare at the paper in his hand.

> *You did remind old Sanford that I'm not quite as good
> at lacrosse as I used to be?* I say.

He gives a grunt.

Mitigating circumstances, he says. *Fortunately you test well, like me.*

I take a deep breath, set down my pen,
and clear my throat.

I'm not applying to Princeton, Dad, I say.
Of course you are, he says.
No, I'm not. I'm applying to schools in Colorado and whichever one takes me, I'm going.

Dad looks at me,
his eyes boring into mine.

Listen son, I didn't raise you to be a quitter. Keep your eye on the prize and you can accomplish anything you set out to.
I'm not quitting anything. I just want to go to school in Colorado.
Because it's easier, because you can get by on minimum effort, he says, moving closer to me, his eyes never leaving mine. *Listen up, Brendan. Here's a quote by an athlete who lost a leg in a roadside bombing in Afghanistan. "You are only limited by the limits you put on yourself."*

I nod.

That's a great quote, Dad. Inspiring. But I've made a

decision. I'm only applying to schools in Colorado.
You're going to Princeton.
I'm not, I say.
Then you're doing it on your own dime.
Fine. I'll get student loans.

We are only about two feet apart
and I can smell his rage.

He wants to hit me so bad it's killing him.
But he can't.

Because of the
wheelchair.

Fine. Pay for Colorado yourself. I'm done, he spits out.

And he stalks out of the room,
slamming the door behind him.

MAXIE

They say it is the coldest winter in
eighty years.
And I believe it.

Colorado is cold,
but in Colorado
you'd get
    12 inches of snow
    and subzero temps
and the next day
it'd be
    40 degrees
    and sunny.

This January in Illinois
the bone-chilling weather is
unrelenting.
Gray frigid day
followed by
gray frigid day.

One day it even plummets to
    25 degrees
    below zero.
Wind chill
    70 below.

They close the public schools
and people are cautioned
to stay indoors.

The North Shore Channel,
a drainage canal
built at the beginning
of the century,
which runs all the way from
Wilmette Harbor
to the
Chicago River
in the city,
freezes solid, the first time
that has happened
in anyone's memory.

In the days that follow,
when the temperature
rises by a few degrees,
but is still double digits
below freezing,
a Mr. Artie Phelps
gets the idea
to set up ice-skating on the
        North Shore Channel.

Mr. Phelps is the type of
fanatical dad
who fills his backyard every winter
with a homemade

skating rink,
for his kids and all the kids
in the neighborhood.

So he takes his mini Zamboni
down to the North Shore Channel,
smoothing
and grooming for a
    good
    long
    way.

My dad is friends with Artie Phelps
and has always been crazy about
ice-skating,
so on a Friday night
he convinces Mom and me
to come check it out.

One of the haiku that
Zander gave me
is about
winter and
cold and
ice,
so even though I'm not a
big ice-skating fan,
I say yes.

A frozen night
skating the North Shore Channel

is about as far as you can get
from a hot summer night
of guns and blood and horror.
And at this point
in my life,
that is a
     very
     good
     thing.

BRENDAN

One of the less obvious and unexpected drawbacks
of being paralyzed is how mind-blowingly cold you get.

Especially when it's
freaking 25 degrees below.

The key, I found out in chat rooms for
us spinal cord injury folks, is layering.

At least three layers,
and I'm talking about indoors.

I've also learned fun stuff like where to keep
my wallet, the best way to insert a catheter,

how to avoid pressure sores,
and if I'll ever have an erection again. (No.)

My dad isn't talking to me much
since I said no to his alma mater.

But my mom surprises me
one afternoon during the cold snap.

I'm in the kitchen, having a sandwich,
when she comes in from bridge.

Instead of giving me the usual kiss on the forehead

and gliding on by, she stops.

She sits at the table with me
and in a soft voice tells me there is money.

Funds in a family trust that have been set aside
for education and she is the executor.

> *It is yours if you need it,* she says, *no matter where you*
> *choose to go.*

I am in shock and don't even have a chance
to respond before she stands,

kisses me on the forehead,
and glides out of the kitchen.

On Friday night I'm working on the application
for University of Colorado.

Suddenly Bobby appears in my doorway,
dangling a pair of ice skates in his hand.

> *Did you hear about the North Shore Channel?* he says.

I shake my head.

> *It's frozen solid and some guy took a Zamboni out on it.*
> *Let's go!*
> *Sorry, bro,* I say, not meeting his eyes, *but I've got these*
> *applications . . .*

You promised, he says. *Besides,* he adds with a big
grin, *I'm pretty sure it's National Take Your Little
Brother Ice-Skating Day.*

And even though the last thing I want to do
is make a fool of myself,

Okay, I say.

MAXIE

I'm amazed by
how many
people there are
gathered at the
        frozen channel.

Word must've spread
and the whole thing
has turned into this
        impromptu
        winter festival.

Someone has set up benches
and there are
torches
as well as a bunch of
bonfires
lining the sides
of the canal.

There is even a
little stand selling
doughnuts
and watery
hot chocolate
with mini marshmallows.

The Bahai Temple,

which during the day
looks like a garish
alien spacecraft
that has landed
in the middle of the Chicago suburbs,
tonight looms over the channel—
a magnificent
and exotic
fairy-tale palace,
all lit up,
 white
 and
 gleaming.

We three skate for a while
and then Mom and I
take a breather.

We are standing by a bonfire
crackling in a large metal garbage bin.
I take photos
of skaters,
with the temple
in the background.

I see Chloe Carney,
pink-cheeked and radiant,
glide by with
a few of her friends.

Dad skates over,

bringing us hot chocolate
and I'm blowing
on mine,
to cool it down
a little,
when Brendan Donnelly
whizzes by.

He is being pushed
in his wheelchair
by a younger guy
who looks like
his little brother.

It is too dark to read
Brendan's face in
the flickering light of
bonfires
and
moonlight,
but his head is thrown back and
he looks different.
        Happy.

I hand Mom my hot chocolate
and hobble back
onto the ice.

Then I take off after Brendan,
camera clutched firmly
in my mittened hand.

The number of people thins out
as I get farther away
from the harbor.
There are
no bonfires
here.

The night is perfectly still,
    the moon
      almost full.

The only sound
I can hear now is
my skates
    cutting
    the
    ice.

The cold wind freezes my face,
but it is exhilarating
swooping along
the glassy smooth surface,
one foot,
then the other,
whoosh whoosh,
like an Olympic speed skater.

At least I feel like I'm going that fast,
but I can't seem
to catch up to
    Brendan and his brother.

A lone torch
marks the spot
where Artie Phelps must've left off his
          grooming.

The ice is rough here,
so I slow down.

I'm beginning to think that
Brendan and his brother
are headed all the way
into Chicago
when I hear voices
ahead of me.

From the torchlight behind
I can just make out
          the wheelchair
          and
          the skater,
and I catch
my breath.

Brendan and his brother
are doing
a figure eight,
in concentric circles,
passing each other
in the middle.

They are awkward

and unpolished,
but it is
an awe-inspiring,
humbling
sight.

And the most beautiful thing
about it is
the concentration and
the joy on
both their faces.

Someone skates up next to me
and I turn to see
     Chloe Carney.

She is intently
watching
the two boys
skate.

Then she turns to me
and smiles.

ANIL

1. The whole point of a shrine,
    I thought, was praying.
    But I have no talent for praying.
    I'm too self-conscious,
    too analytical.
    My prayers tend to be
    more like checklists,
    or mathematical formulas.

2. My mom says there is
    no right way to pray
    and that prayer is really just
    thinking.
    Focused thinking perhaps.
    Anyway, it's not like I kneel
    in front of my dresser and pray.

    More often, I lie on my bed,
    glancing over at the pieces of glass,
    the roses, and the candle,
    and yes, up at those
    glow-in-the-dark stars
    pasted on the ceiling,
    which have become an
    unofficial part of my shrine.

3. My mother has already started

planning the feast that she will cook
for the Hindu festival of Holi
which in India marks the
start of spring.
It always falls on
the day of the first full moon
in March, which this year
is on the 19th.

Holi is also called
the Festival of Colors.
At night people light bonfires
to say good-bye to winter.
They gather together to
sing and dance and play music.
And during the day they throw
gulal at each other—
brightly colored powders
that you carry in your pocket
to fling at anyone
you meet.

Everyone knows to wear
old clothes on Holi because
the *gulal* will stain.
By the end of the day
everyone is covered with
brilliant colored splotches—
on hair, faces, eyelashes, lips,
clothes, shoes.
Like they've been tie-dyed.

I love photos of Holi,
the laughter on everyone's face.
As if they're throwing
Technicolor clouds of happiness
into the air.
Anointing
everyone around them
with color.

4.   I still think about Maxie.
In a different universe,
I imagine spending Holi with her,
us laughing together,
drenched in color.

But she has made it clear that
I am an outcast to her, that
we cannot be friends.
And sometimes I do not know
if I can recover from that.

If I could wash away
these feelings, the way you can
cleanse yourself of the *gulal* powders
at the end of Holi, I would.

But what kind of unholy joke is it
that I should have stumbled across
this stubbornly unyielding joy
in a girl's crooked smile
on that one terrible night.

POLICE CHIEF AUBREY DELAFIELD

When it looked like one of those kids
was going to die,
the prosecutor was all set
to slap Walter Smith with
Murder One.

But as soon as the boy who lost an eye
came out of the coma,
things shifted.

There was plenty of talk.

That Walter Smith was on suicide watch,
        which I knew to be true, early on anyway.
That his court-assigned lawyer was going
        to plead not guilty by reason of insanity.
That he was going to plead not guilty period,
        using a defense similar to the 'Stand Your Ground' laws
        they've got in states like Arizona and Alabama,
        under the theory that he had a legitimate fear of
        being under attack.

Then on a cold morning in April,
word came down that Walter Smith was going
to plead guilty.

A plea bargain had been reached,

second-degree murder,
with a possible sentence of eight to nineteen years in prison,
depending on the judge's final decision.

I wondered why Walter decided
to plead guilty.
I heard it was against the advice of his lawyer.

My best guess is it had to do with
all those tears I saw him shed
that night,
on the curb
and at the jail.

I remember thinking at the time that
he was like a kid who had done something wrong,
and knew it,
and felt bad.

WALTER

When a marshal is hired to protect a town but it turns out
    the town is populated by the lawless and the insane,
the only option left for the sheriff is to
    turn in his badge.

EMMA

We get a call from the prosecutor
saying that Walter Smith
is going to plead guilty.

He asks if we want
to attend the hearing,
maybe even say something to the judge.

Faith isn't sure she wants to go.
But I am sure. Which is surprising
because lately there has been very little I'm sure of.

EMMA

The day of the hearing, Faith
decides to come with me, even
though I told her she didn't have to.

Anil is the only other one of us there.
He is with his parents and seeing him
in the courtroom is somehow comforting.

Chloe told me Brendan refused to come, mainly because
his dad wanted him to, wanted everyone in the courtroom
to see Brendan in his wheelchair.

Brendan's dad thought that their seeing the wheelchair
would get Walter Smith slapped in jail for
the maximum sentence allowed by the law.

Chloe says that Brendan's turned a corner.
He's more interested in looking ahead than looking back.
And that he doesn't care what his dad wants.

I stare at Walter Smith, who looks so small and pale
in his oversize glasses, and all I can think is that he
looks like one of those scrawny stubby-tailed squirrels,

the ones you see frozen in the middle of the road
as your car barrels toward them, and you know
that squirrel isn't long for this world.

And suddenly I know
I have to say something.
Something important.

When the prosecutor looks over at me,
I stand up. My hands are shaking
and my tongue feels thick in my mouth.

I start to talk but only a
croaking sound comes out. The judge
asks me to speak up.

I clear my throat,
take a deep breath
and this time my voice is loud, clear.

We were all at fault, I say. *Not just Walter Smith.*
We were all to blame.

WALTER SMITH

When the girl with the dark-red ponytail stands up to speak
    I realize she is the sister of the girl with the dog,
the one on the bike. They look a little alike,
    but this one has a harder face, not as nice-looking.

But then I notice her hands are shaking,
    and what she says surprises me.
She says everything that happened that night
    wasn't just my fault. We were all to blame.

And I suddenly remember the movie *High Noon* and how
    the marshal's nice wife who wears white dresses
is the only one in the whole town who helps the marshal,
    who stands beside him when the bad guys come.

The girl with the pony tail now has tears running
    down her cheeks, and she turns toward me
looks me straight in the eye.
    And she says, "I'm sorry."

Tears are running out of my eyes, too, and then
    a man with a red face jumps up and starts yelling
about how his son is crippled for life because of
    "that sonofabitch" and I realize he means me.

The judge bangs her gavel, telling the man to be quiet.
    He won't and so a sheriff takes him away.

I look at the ponytail girl, sitting next to her sister.
They are holding hands and looking back at me.

And my heart starts beating hard because just for a second
I think that maybe there still are good guys
in this world. And that maybe I shouldn't
hand in my badge after all.

MAXIE

It is a warm Saturday in
early July.
Mom is in the kitchen,
trying a new recipe for turkey chili,
and Dad is off at the garden center.
Now that he's got a job,
Dad wants to get the backyard
      fixed up.

The doorbell rings.
I open the door
and Anil Sayanantham
      is
      standing
      there.

Right away I can't
breathe.

> *Hi, Maxie,* he says.
> *Hi,* I half whisper, half say.
> *How are you?* he asks.

I stammer back that I'm okay.
Which,
despite my current inability
to breathe,

is actually sort of
  true.

  Uh, he starts, then clears his throat. *I've been wanting*
    to tell you that those photos you took, the ones in
    Versions, *were amazing. Congratulations on getting*
    the Ellen Loomis Award. You deserved it.
  Thanks, I manage to reply.

This is so surreal,
I think to myself,
chitchatting on the front
stoop
with Anil Sayanantham.

  I heard you're going to Columbia, I say.
  Well, yes and no, he says, *I'm actually taking a year off.*
    Going to India to live with my mom's family. Work in
    a clinic, travel.
  Wow, that's great, I say.
  How about you, next year I mean?
  Uh, not India exactly, but I did get into Northwestern,
    which is sort of a miracle.

I hear my mom calling me
from inside
the house.

  Well, I say, *it was nice to see you, but I . . .*
  Maxie, Anil blurts out, his cinnamon-colored skin
    tinged with a red blush, *I was wondering, if you,*

well, would like to go to dinner with me next Saturday
night? And maybe a movie?

I am
floored.

Is Anil Sayanantham
actually asking me out
    on a
    date?

Really?
Like nothing ever happened?
Like somehow we are
just a normal
    teenage boy
    and
    teenage girl?

I can't take it in.
I feel tears brimming up
in my eyes.

Because
Anil <u>is</u>
    that night.

I stare at him.

But then I think to myself
that Chloe

and Brendan
and Emma
and Faith
and Felix
are all
     that night.

All of us.

And suddenly it's like a
giant bank of klieg lights
flashes on
in my head.

Anil is also
now,
and
here,
in my front doorway,
asking me out on
     a date.

So is it possible that maybe,
just maybe,
<u>Anil</u> might be
a new now time,
like in Joey Pigza,
that bit I was reading Felix
when he
woke
up?

Anil is looking at me,
intently,
watching my face
as if his
entire life
depended on
my
answer.

Then he suddenly says,

    Oh wait . . .

and digs into his pocket.
He pulls out something small
and puts it
    in my hand.

I look down at what lies
in my palm.
A piece of frosty green
sea glass.

Then I look back up at him
    and smile.

He smiles back,
that great shining smile of his
I'd almost forgotten,
and all at once
I can

breathe
again.

In fact, I feel light and radiant,
like a thousand tiny suns
are shining
in my heart.

Yes, I say.

ANIL

1. I feel as if *gulal* has just been
   thrown all over me.
   That I am drenched
   with color.
   A walking talking
   incarnation of
   radiant
   Technicolor.

   Tie-dyed.
   Anointed.
   Happy.

EMMA

We are at Gillson Beach,
the three of us,
Max, Felix, and me.

It is about five o'clock
on a hot, but not too hot,
evening in July.

Most of the sunbathers and
swimmers have gone home,
but the smell of suntan lotion lingers.

The sand is still warm and I dig
my toes in, gazing down at the
webbing of scars on my right leg.

We're up at the top of the beach,
where the grassy area
meets the sand.

And we're sitting on a blanket, eating
guacamole Felix made. He's still obsessed
with guacamole, which is okay by me.

> *I have a date this weekend,* Maxie says out of the blue.
> *What?* I say, not sure I heard right.
> *A date, with Anil Sayanantham,* she says.

About time, says Felix, giving Maxie a high five.
Well, hey, that's great, I say, surprised, but at the same
    time happy for her.

Then I lie back on the blanket,
closing my eyes and listening to the
steady gentle sound of waves on the sand.

I can feel Maxie get up off the blanket,
then hear the click of her camera, and I open my eyes,
to see what she's taking a photo of.

She's pointing her camera at a bur oak tree,
and sitting on one of the branches,
is a black bird. A crow.

And for just a second my vision goes red.
I see blood smearing the surface of
Polly's rubber crow, and I start to shake.

Emma? comes Felix's voice.
Oh God, I'm sorry, cries Maxie, instantly lowering her
    camera. *I didn't think . . .*

Felix reaches over
and takes my hand.
His is warm, reassuring.

It's okay, he says, his voice definite. *Crows are
beautiful, Emma. Smart and strong. Survivors. Like us.*

MAXIE

Emma is eating
a brownie,
and Felix is reading
a book out loud to her,
>not Joey Pigza but some
>new book of poetry he's
>obsessed with,
>about a
>hidden driveway.

It must be funny because
they're both laughing
a lot.

I wander down to
the water and walk
along the shoreline.
I am clutching the piece of
>sea glass Anil gave me.

I come to this intersection
of sand and a long promontory
of rocks
that juts out
into the lake
and spot something large-ish
>sticking up
>out of the sand.

I think it's just a big rock
that's fallen
off the seawall,
but when I look closer
I see I'm wrong.

Not quite believing
what I'm seeing,
I whip out
        my camera.

Lodged in the sand,
its head at an angle,
is a stone statue.

It is worn and faded
and streaked with
seaweed and lichen,
but I can clearly see that it is a
        garden gnome.

I start taking photos
from different angles,
and am so absorbed that I
don't even notice when
Felix and Emma
come up behind me.

We wondered what you found, says Emma.

They peer at the gnome.

Excellent, says Felix, bursting out laughing.

And the three of us
sit in a semicircle
around it
while I take a few more
photos.

> *I kind of remember reading about this,* says Emma,
> *in the town paper, about a bunch of statues that*
> *were stolen from people's yards and then buried in*
> *the sand at Gillson Beach. Some middle school boys*
> *playing a prank. It was last summer, back before . . . ,*
> she trails off.
> *Yeah, I remember,* I say.

I gaze at the gnome
and think how he must've gotten
washed out
into the lake,
but the tide finally
        brought him back
        to shore.

And then I look at
        Emma's leg,
        Felix's fake eye,
and even into
        my own fragile but healing heart
and think that somehow it all
fits together.

We fit together.
EMFAX.
    On this day.
    On this beach.
    With this garden gnome.
    In this new now time.

Acknowledgments

It has been a long road back and here is who I want to thank:

MELANIE, my editor and own personal white bird miracle, who said yes and asked all the right questions. I can't imagine a finer travel companion.

RUBIN, agent extraordinaire, who took the train from Boston, bought me a Cobb salad, and told me what he would do. And he did it, with persistence, creativity, and grace.

DAVID and JACK, for bringing me back to life that night in the labyrinthine Italian restaurant. And also to Jack for his good will about using Joey Pigza. I know it's the way I'd want to wake up from a coma.

CILLE, cousin/sister/best friend, who always believed.

VITA and MATT, who read the manuscript side by side in the sunroom and gave me two thumbs-up. And also to Matt for turning me on to the Poetry Foundation app.

TIM, for giving the green light, being glad to see me back, and for his excellent taste in music.

MICHAEL, former editor, former agent, and still dearest pal, for sending me pics of Aidan Quinn and for still making me laugh.

MIRIAM, who deftly guided me through the home stretch with patience, wisdom and a keen eye.

MY OHYA LADIES—Erin, Linda, Lisa, Margaret, Rae, Natalie, and Julia—whose support and good cheer have meant the world to me.

MY TROL LADIES—Beth, Carol, Claudia, the other Edie, Kristen, Lorrie, Nancianne, Sandy, and Sylvia—amazing librarians, teachers, and passionate champions of children's literature.

DRS. TIM RICHARDS and CHRIS SAUNDERS, for their impeccable consultation on all things medical.

CHARLES, for being my first reader and best friend.

EDITH PATTOU is the author of the *New York Times* bestselling picture book, *Mrs. Spitzer's Garden,* as well as three award-winning fantasy novels for young adults, including *East,* which was chosen one of the "100 Best of the Best Young Adult Books for the 21st Century" by the Young Adult Library Association. It was also selected an ALA Top Ten Best Book for Young Adults, an ALA Notable Children's Book, and a *School Library Journal* Best Book of the Year. A former librarian and bookseller, Edith Pattou lives in Columbus, Ohio. You can visit her at www.edithpattou.com